DOOMSDAY MESA

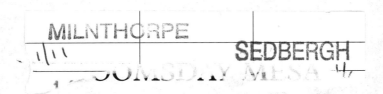
Ex-cavalryman Yale Cannon rode to Antelope for two very different reasons – in search of an old sweetheart and to bring out Red Effingham, a gunslick killer the sheriff had locked up in the ranch town's jailhouse – so he decided to use one mission as cover for the other. His delving for old time's sake quickly met opposition, but introduced him to suffragist schoolteacher Kate McDowell. Kate revealed that hatred between the cowmen and a settler community led by Abel Pryor, religious fanatic, was coming to a showdown. With Effingham busted from jail, the clash was set to be violent and bloody!

DOOMSDAY MESA

by

Chap O'Keefe

Dales Large Print Books
Long Preston, North Yorkshire,
BD23 4ND, England.

British Library Cataloguing in Publication Data.

O'Keefe, Chap
    Doomsday mesa.

    A catalogue record of this book is
    available from the British Library

    ISBN   978-1-84262-789-1 pbk

First published in Great Britain in 1995 by Robert Hale Limited

Published in Large Print 2011 by arrangement with
Keith Chapman

Dales Large Print is an imprint of Library Magna Books Ltd.

Printed and bound in Great Britain by
T.J. (International) Ltd., Cornwall, PL28 8RW

1

'Living by the Gun...'

At age twenty Yale Cannon was nothing much. Call him an adventurer at best ... though others would have had it he was just a hell-raising kid, with some gun trouble down his back-trail and talk of a killing in Independence, Missouri. The War Between the States had barely begun, and Cannon hadn't seen fit to enlist. So the impressive Army career – four years of fighting for the Union and two years campaigning in the south-west against the Indians – still lay in an unthought-of future.

He joined the wagon train like he did most things, on the spur of the moment and with no clear goal except maybe to satisfy the restless urge for a changing horizon and to escape the pursuing shadows of retribution for past escapades. He would cross the Great Plains, sharing the gamble and the dream of the emigrant families gripped by the magnet of the virgin lands of the West.

On the wagon train were people unlike himself in that they had an ambition in life and the will to pursue it. But here was the promise of action for sure, and the young Yale Cannon was never happier than when he was in the thick of life's battle.

And if it needed more than that, there was the girl.

She was purely the neatest thing he'd ever seen. Her name was Jane Bell and she was travelling with her pa and ma. She had large, beautiful eyes, blue as forget-me-nots, and her hair was the colour of copper and tumbled in ringlets to her shoulders. She had small hands and feet and was a little above medium height. Her complexion was taking on a fetching, golden tan from long hours in the sun.

For her, Yale Cannon could stomach

anything. Even the dust. Even Luther Smith.

The dust was churned up in a powdery white fog by the wheels of the heavily laden wagons and the hoofs of the oxen teams plodding to cover their twenty miles a day. It was insidious stuff. It coated the canvas covers of the wagons and sifted through everything. Stored rations were contaminated. It seeped down collars inside the trekkers' clothing, and crusted the nostrils and lips of man and beast whose airways it invaded.

Luther Smith was an aggravation of another kind. Not much older than Yale, he knew it all. Much of his wisdom was drawn from a battered, dog-eared emigrants' guidebook stuffed in his trousers' back pocket.

Unlike Cannon, Smith had his own wagon and regarded Cannon – with just his buckskin stallion, his saddle, its bags, his bedroll and his guns – as nothing more than a hanger-on. Sure, he acknowledged Cannon knew how to use his Henry rifle. But 'newfangled' was what he called it with a con-temptuous curl of his thin lips.

The lever-action repeater had a tube magazine below the barrel, and was made to hold fifteen .44 calibre rim-fire cartridges. With one cartridge in the chamber, that gave Cannon sixteen shots and a distinct edge when the emigrants had call for a little fresh meat.

Smith chose to disregard that Cannon was also the best hunter among them. Nor did he care to consider the worth Cannon's Henry rifle and his skill with it might prove if they were beset by Indians before their journey was done.

To cap everything, Luther Smith was also sweet on Jane Bell.

The incident that brought the friction between Cannon and Smith to a climax was ostensibly a row over Smith's guidebook. The wagons were circled, the campfire was ablaze and night was falling fast.

'According to the description of our route, we'll soon get shuck of this damned desert dust. Yonder aways, the dry country ends. The facts are in here,' Smith said, sitting on the tongue of his wagon and tapping the title page of his opened book.

'All necessary information relative to the equipment, supplies, and the method of travelling,' he quoted. 'By Lansford W. Hastings. Cincinnati, 1845.'

Smith's complacency irked Cannon. He banged his hat against his thigh, dislodging the caked dust from the brim, and scoffed.

'Who in the world 'cept a greenhorn would take that tomfoolishness for gospel? I'd rather palaver with the mountain men and the old-time missionaries who blazed the trails. 'Sides, I seem to recall a copy of that very same volume played a part in the Donner Party tragedy back in 'forty-six, 'forty-seven. Forty-four lives lost on account of following your Mr Hastings' advice.'

'Are you trying to discredit the guidebook, kid?' Smith asked. His mouth had tightened and Cannon shrewdly observed that the audience included Jane Bell.

'I figure I ain't much more of a kid than your own self, Luther Smith,' said Cannon, resenting the way he'd been addressed. 'Moreover, I know there's more to the world than book learning.'

Blood rose under Smith's skin, congesting his face. Still gripping the book, he shook his fist at Cannon.

'Blasted upstart saddle-bum!' he snarled. 'Have a care to mind your lip! I seen your game. Trying to put me down and raise your own stock ... making up to Miss Bell and her folks on the sly! Well, they ain't your kind, killer!'

Cannon didn't hesitate – not even to check whether pretty Jane Bell was excited, horrified or scandalized by this revelatory exchange of ill-tempered words. Maybe he was too hot and tired, too saddle-weary to tolerate one jot more of Luther Smith's overbearing ways and gratuitous insults. Maybe he was tempted by the target of the flourished guidebook.

Whatever, he snatched a revolver from a

tied-down holster.

One thing young Cannon didn't stint himself on was guns. The handgun, in common with the Henry rifle, was the latest type generally available, a Model 1860 Army in .44 calibre.

The slug punched a ragged hole straight through the centre of the Lansford Hastings guidebook, tearing it from Smith's grasp and hurling it to the ground.

The sharp explosion of the percussion cap brought a sudden stillness and the astonished attention of the whole camp. Then Smith spat a string of profane oaths. He clutched his emptied left hand as though expecting it to be ruined for all time.

Finding it wasn't, his right swooped for the pistol at his own belt.

In the same instant, wagonmaster Bull Hammond let out an angry roar. He was a mean cuss at the best of times – mighty mean – and he kept a close rein on what went on among his pilgrims. He didn't hold with slacking, immoderate drinking or fighting in his camp.

Least of all, gunfighting.

Powerfully built and stocky, he stamped fearlessly into the space between the two young men.

'All right, you fellers! That does it!' Hammond's voice was tight and hard. 'You're through with this train. I'm throwin' you all off, you hear me? You got till mornin' to light the hell outa here, preferably in diff'rent directions, keepin' offa my route an' well outa my hair!'

'Where's the justice in that, Mr Hammond?' Cannon objected.

'Don't talk in that tone to me, boy!'

'If you heard what happened, you'd know Smith was plumb asking for it – stirring trouble, calling me names,' Cannon pressed on. 'What's in a man's past is his own affair. The West is the place you start over. It's what you do, not what you were, that matters. The slate is wiped off.'

Bull Hammond growled and was obdurate. 'Mebbe, young man. But that sure was awful fancy shootin'.'

Cannon jerked his head challengingly, lifted his square chin.

'What of it? I shot to teach him a lesson. Not to *kill* him. I aimed at his pesky book, and hit it dead centre with the one shot.'

'Sure you did. Fast and accurate. Too much so. You don't get that good less'n there's a trail behind you someplace. It makes me uncomf'table, mister.'

Cannon shrugged. 'I thought you folks could use a good marksman. I can hunt. I can fight Indians if the need arises.'

The wagonmaster would have no part of the argument. He jabbed a broken-nailed, stubby finger in the air to give his words emphasis.

'Them that do their livin' by the gun is apt to do their dyin' by it likewise. What's more, innocent folks get dragged in an' hurt. I seen it happen often-times – an' I ain't abidin' it!'

'You're a hard man and a stubborn one, Mr Hammond.'

'You're quittin', you hear? That's flat and

final, Cannon!'

'So be it, sir! I can see what I say counts for nothing hereabouts.'

'Not with me it don't.'

But before he left Cannon privately sought out Jane Bell. Maybe he shouldn't be too eager to take out, irritated and restless though he felt. Jane was no average girl. She had a quiet distinction not ordinarily found in the young ladies he'd encountered west of the Missouri. Yet they had secretly shared some very close moments together and he felt he could justifiably assume she would be deeply offended if he were to ride away without a word.

He found her alone, down a path through some low, wind-broken oaks and brush, in a narrow draw cut by a river presently shrunk to a sluggish trickle. Whether the privacy was a matter of luck or her own fixing, he couldn't rightly figure.

To his consternation, her beautiful blue eyes were filled with distress. And it was not, apparently, the thought of his imminent banishment that occasioned it.

'You must do as you see fit, Yale,' she told him with a coldness to which he was un-accustomed. 'I cannot let myself stand in your way. You may consider yourself dis-charged. Perhaps you are, after all, no more than what they say – a common shootist. A man who guns down others less capable than himself!'

Yale was momentarily speechless. For an instant, he felt tears prick in his own eyes, thinking of all he had thought was and might have been.

He looked down quickly, and when he looked up he had blinked the wateriness away. He groped for words that once spoken he knew were inadequate.

'I thought we *knew* each other, Jane. I didn't mean to give you offence. Nor did I ever think you'd turn against me.'

She turned her face from him with a toss of her brush-burnished curls. 'I'm only very young, Yale Cannon! I don't know every-thing, nor even always what I should do, lest it be to listen to my elders – to my folks and Mr Hammond.'

Though it was something he didn't then recognize, Yale was very young, too. His pride was hurt. Foolishness, fuss, recriminations, tears ... all these things he sensed were so close were also things he feared more, in a way, than the kind of disagreement that could be settled with action and ultimately a quick exchange of gunfire.

He shrugged. 'I'm not a quarrelsome man, Jane, and I never stirred up any trouble on purpose, nor killed anybody that wasn't asking for it. All my gunfights have been fair and square. But I reckon you talk like you were on Luther Smith's side.'

'I'm on nobody's side!'

He didn't understand her exasperation. 'That means you aren't on mine. I'm sorry, Jane. I guess they're right and I should be getting along. You and me aren't cut from the same cloth.'

'Yale, you have no idea...'

'Well, no matter. Could be I was imagining things, sorta taking it for granted you'd admire to have me riding with you beside the Bell wagon. Maybe I should go where the fighting is – this War Between the States they talk of.'

She still kept her back to him, so he shrugged again and walked away, not even saying goodbye.

But as he went he felt her eyes staring after him until he was gone through the clump of stunted oaks.

Two decades rolled by and the early years of a third. In the wider world, Austrians and Italians, Prussians and French, waged wars of their own. The Suez Canal was opened. Count Leo Tolstoy published his major works *War and Peace* and *Anna Karenina,* and the century's most popular novelist, Charles Dickens, died. The Queen of England was declared Empress of India and the scientific wonder of electric lighting was introduced. More war was waged on the tide of empire in faraway places ... in the Soudan,

Afghanistan and Zululand.

In North America, General Lee surrendered to General Grant at Appomattox, Virginia, and civil war was succeeded by Indian wars and the rapid extermination of the buffalo, upon which much of Indian life depended. The first transcontinental railroad – 1,848 miles of track – was completed by Central Pacific building eastward from Sacramento, California, and Union Pacific building westward from Omaha, Nebraska; a golden spike was hammered into the last wooden tie.

It was the age, too, of the cattle kingdom and great drovers' trails. Like the mighty Chisholm, north the thousand dangerous miles from Texas to the stockyards and railhead of Abilene, Kansas – a rip-roaring, wide open town till the moral reformers, farming interests and urban businessmen banded together and forced the cattle trade and its parasites to find new havens in Wichita and Dodge City.

Meanwhile, Yale Cannon distinguished

himself as a soldier. Decorated for his bravery in battle, respected for his loyalty to the Stars and Stripes, Captain Cannon was a popular if reticent subject for both the eastern and the frontier Press, whose hacks were never loath to exaggerate in detailing his daring exploits against guerrilla rebels and Indian savages.

The years of army service, during the war and the campaigns in the south-west, made him a perfect pick after his retirement from the military for a prized federal commission. His allegiance was unquestionable. He took up duties as Deputy Marshal Cannon.

Mostly, the work was routine, doing the legwork of the civil and criminal courts of the United States. Such posts as Cannon's and his superiors' were routinely awarded on a patronage basis to an assortment of politicians, merchants, lawyers and others with connections to high office. Financial reward came in the form of fees for specific legal services and payment of expenses. Ordinarily, and frequently between holding down secondary jobs, federal marshals' deputies issued and served subpoenas, located witnesses and executed writs and warrants.

Less ordinarily, the capture of outlaws and criminal investigations were involved. Field duties could therefore be reliably entrusted only to those with experience in frontier communities and on the wilderness trails – and with the proven capacity for independent and courageous action.

Here it was that Deputy Marshal Cannon came into his own, bringing his abilities to bear and extending his reputation.

A spring day in his forties found him a grey-haired, mature gent of quiet confidence and dignity, yet soldierly in his bearing and still the man of action with swift responses and nerves of steel.

It also found him riding the stage road to a small town called Antelope. Official business awaited him there, but so did the unofficial.

For the past was a burial ground for secrets and regrets, and Yale Cannon had his private, sentimental reasons for being glad of the excuse to travel to this neck of the woods, where he hoped to uncover some facts, maybe lay a few ghosts…

2

Stolen Beef

Beneath a darkening afternoon sky, Yale Cannon rode straight-backed like the military man he had been. His clean-limbed steeldust was a powerful horse with a lot of guts and eager to go. But he held the mount in check to a pace he knew it had the stamina to maintain, though he wasted no time.

He'd ridden from earliest dawn and toward noon he'd observed a ceiling of cloud pushing in across the blue with a strong wind behind it. Eventually, he assessed, the clouds would spill and for several hours it would rain – mean, needle-sharp, and promising to make life miserable for the rider and horse who did not complete their journeying ahead of it.

He could do without such discomforts. For a man of his age, he led a life that was hard and lonely enough – the more so, it seemed, as he grew older. He was fooling himself for certain sure, but it did no harm to dream that in Antelope he could trace something that might make him feel a little less of a loner. He needed the reminder that it hadn't always been so, and that it wasn't a status entirely of his own choice.

The steeldust's low-throated snort was the first indication to Cannon that anything was wrong along the lonesome trail into Antelope. It was rolling country, with the inclines sporadically concealing what might lie uptrail or to either side.

Cannon drew rein and listened.

The terrain sloped steeply down to the right and was grown with cottonwoods, as though a stream might run at the bottom. Rising from behind the trees, but blown away by the stiffening breeze, came the bawling of cattle.

The steeldust's alert ears pointed toward the screening trees and he repeated his snort and danced aside.

'I don't know, Steely,' Cannon said to the beast. 'I don't know about this at all. Spooked cattle ain't none of our business, and the weather is closing in on us, but maybe we should go take a look-see.'

He turned off the trail and steered the sure-footed steeldust between the dead and living trees downhill. Occasionally, they leaped fallen timber blocking their path, and as they went the bawling became more distinct.

'Only one thing makes beeves take on so,' said Cannon. 'And that's death!'

They came out onto lush grass, a natural meadow, and the steeldust balked.

A small bunch of cattle was gathered there, pawing and bellowing around some darkish heap on the ground. The cattle, Cannon noted, were mixed stuff, part of an

25

improved herd – mostly crosses between inferior Texas longhorns and imported breeding stock, shorthorns, probably from the eastern states. The adult animals would weigh between 1,000 and 1,200 pounds a head, Cannon judged, and they carried a Crazy-P brand on their left flanks.

He stepped down from the saddle and moved in closer, warily, ready to run back and leap into the saddle. One of the cows tossed its head and snorted wildly. Cannon sensed the critter was not specially vicious, just infected with unreasoning fear. Its boggling eyes were black, glistening balls.

Cannon took off his broad, pearl-coloured stetson and flapped it at the bunch. 'Move! Scat!'

To his relief, the cranky cattle backed up, then turned as a unit and ran off a short way in stiff-legged terror. The bulls acted as sentinels bringing up the rear, bellowing but showing no desire to charge.

Cannon saw why. The dread of blood and slaughter was upon them. The object around which they'd grouped was a plump black heifer, less than a yearling, maybe six months old.

A pool of blood stained the grass stickily where the young cow's throat had been slit. The hindquarters had been hacked off the carcass and removed from the scene. The stench from this crude butchery hung in the air and swarms of big black flies set up a constant buzzing.

Long experience had tuned Cannon's eyes and ears for the slightest development in any situation. A sudden stirring of dust and the faint drumming of hoofs caused Cannon to look up. Two riders appeared, skylined on the rim at the far side of the hollow.

One of the horsemen shouted and pointed at him.

'Now what's biting on these fellers?' Cannon asked himself.

The pair descended pell-mell, bringing their horses to slithering halts, one behind, one in front of Cannon. His steeldust, who had been cropping grass nearby unconcernedly, lifted his head and nickered a greeting at the panting newcomers.

'Good day, gentlemen. What's the rush?' Cannon asked, keeping his manner courteous.

'Caught red-handed!' the younger of the two men snarled. 'Killin' our calves, you sonofabitch!'

'Poppycock! Do I look like I've blood on my hands?'

Cannon spread his arms, the open gesture inviting his accosters to examine the fine but trail-dusty suit of black, the white shirt and tidily knotted string tie, the stetson he still held in one big fist.

But the pair were on the prod and not ready to give up the mistaken assumption he was in some wise implicated in stealing their beef.

They turned to one another, and Cannon read the looks they exchanged and a whole lot more, as was his practised way. Physical similarities marked them as kin, possibly brothers. They had the same rugged stamp and dark, curly hair poking out under their hat brims, but it ended there.

The elder had the beginnings of worry lines between his brows and furrowing his brow, though Cannon put his age as under thirty. A battler, he thought, getting care-worn. Hard-working but maybe to the degree where he'd gotten out of the habit of taking the time to think things through.

The younger was surly, with a shifty cast to his eyes, and gave Cannon a less favour-able impression. At bottom, he was prob-ably the weaker of the two as well as the junior, yet this somehow also made him the more dangerous.

'I say he ain't on the level, Dallas,' the young man said. 'Snoopin' round our stock. He knows somethin' 'bout this. Or his friends do. I reckon you should l'arn him a lesson!' He gave Cannon a vicious glare.

The man addressed as Dallas heaved a sigh. He swept Cannon from head to foot with a tired eye, taking in his garb.

'You ain't no range-rider, mister. I figger

you might be another convert headed for that Bible-punchin' crowd of hoemen on the mesa – them that's been rustlin' our stock!'

'*Your* stock?' Cannon prompted quietly, jabbing a questioning thumb toward the bunch of edgy cattle.

'Sure. I'm Dallas Perigo, boss of the Crazy-P, and this here's my kid brother Mel.'

'Fergit the *kid*, Dallas!' Mel Perigo snapped. 'We don't owe this turkey no explanations.' His free hand clutched hard at the saddle pommel, the other swung the loose rein ends, and he showed his teeth. 'I say we run him off – but fast. Mebbe we c'n get him shiftin' with some slugs in his boot heels. It'll show him who asks the questions an' gives the orders around here!'

Mel's right hand suddenly moved from the pommel, grabbing for the six-shooter at his lean hip.

When a man was about to draw a gun on you, the time for being mild was over.

Cannon's right hand darted across his chest to his left armpit where he carried a Colt in a shoulder harness under his coat. As Mel Perigo's gun cleared the holster, he fired.

Though the Perigos didn't know who he was, Cannon had once held a reputation for his draw and his marksmanship. The slug lifted the high-crowned hat off the kid's head.

Mel's horse, startled, reared wildly. The youngster lost both his gun and his balance and was pitched from the saddle hard onto his backside in the grass.

'Damn you!' he screeched. 'A sneaking hideout rig! Dallas'll kill you for this!'

Cannon's tone was heavy; he felt kind of weary. 'Kid, you're a young fool. You asked for it, and you came mighty close to getting it!'

Dallas Perigo looked more unhappy than ever. Whatever his brother said, he'd clearly no stomach for a shootout with someone as fast and accurate as Yale Cannon. The store clothes had maybe misled the Perigos into

31

the false assumption he was a greenhorn as well as a stranger. But Dallas was looking at Cannon again now, surely seeing the things they should have observed before...

Cannon had a tough face with skin weathered near mahogany by long years under open skies; the ends of his moustache were sun-bleached. No thinking man could mistake him for a soft easterner with looks like those.

Dallas spoke up. 'We told you who we are, and we've been missin' cattle. We can't take kindly to strangers hornin' in on our range.' He inquired sharply, making it a challenge, 'What's your handle, mister, and what's your business?'

Cannon sensed the pose the rancher struck was more to save some face for his brother than to bolster his own ego.

'The name's Cannon and I was riding to Antelope when I heard your cattle bawling.'

Dallas nodded, digesting this. 'Why to Antelope, Mr Cannon? It's no more'n a cow town an' ain't much of a place, 'cept to us ranchin' folks who use it for a tradin' post.'

Cannon hesitated, but only slightly, before he replied.

'I've some friends in this section. That is, I heard they settled hereabouts way back.'

'Who are they?'

'Their name was Bell. It was at the time of the War Between the States.'

Mel, who'd picked himself up and was quieting his restive mount, butted in. 'Bell? I ain't heard o' no Bells, Dallas. Sounds like hogwash to me.'

'Button your lip, Mel!' Dallas said testily. 'We seen enough fightin' for one day.'

He turned back to Cannon. 'My brother's right. We know most ev'ryone around 'cept those Pryorite newcomers on the mesa, an' there ain't no Bells.'

Cannon shrugged. 'Well, I got to say again it was way back...'

'Yeah. I was jest a shirt-tail kid if it was when you says.'

'What about your elder folks – your pa and ma maybe?'

'Pa's been under the ground these past five years, an' ma's grown kinda sick and forgetful. Talk of the old days upsets her. She don't like to chinwag 'bout it.'

'Oh, I see...'

Dallas laughed bitterly. 'Prob'ly not.' He pushed his hat back on his head. After briefly pondering, he added, 'It's like this. There ain't nearly nobody been livin' round Antelope that long, an' the few that has don't talk 'bout it no more. The old-timers first in here was killed by Injuns – leastways, nigh on ev'ry man jack of 'em. The Cheyenne did it after the Sand Creek Massacre of sixty-four.'

Cannon was familiar with the broad facts of the incident. In 1864, the Third Colorado Volunteers under Colonel John Chivington had deviously and ruthlessly attacked the sleeping Cheyenne reservation on Sand Creek, killing more than two hundred tribespeople, many of them women and children. In an ugly demonstration of their 'victory', the volunteers had displayed Indian scalps and severed genitals to cheering crowds in Denver.

Cheyenne retaliation had been swift and equally brutal. Towns, ranches and way stations were sacked with a vengeance, and travel across the Plains to Denver had to be stopped.

From all standpoints, it was a chapter of American history best buried.

'Old Antelope was put to the torch – twice,' Dallas Perigo said grimly.

Cannon shook his head and tutted. 'Bad. Can't say's I blame folks for wanting to forget. But there must be somebody from the old days...'

'Let him pester ol' McDowell,' Mel piped up. 'The ornery wiseacre reck'ns he was here at the start. He was one of 'em the Injuns didn't wipe out, more's the pity!'

Dallas frowned. 'That's no way to talk about the reverend, Mel. Have some respect! He's Rose's father an' I figgered you had ambitions in that direction,'

Mel smirked. 'No more'n you got your eye

on her sister Kate!'

Dallas' skin darkened and he stiffened, but he let the retort pass. 'The Reverend McDowell is the preacher in Antelope, Mr Cannon,' he explained. 'He has two – uh – right pretty daughters. He's also the last survivor of the town's pioneer days. He's getting along in years now, but he's the kind of minister who never abandons his flock, I guess, an' Kate, who teaches school, is a big help to him.'

'Yeah, Kate pretty much runs things in the sky-pilotin' line an' most ev'ry other besides,' Mel said. There was a hint of sarcasm in the words Cannon didn't especially like. 'Has a down on me though, 'cos I'm the bad boy who's taken a shine to her little sister.'

'Shuddup, Mel,' Dallas said, losing patience. 'That ain't neither here nor there.' Again he swung his attention back to Cannon. 'My brother is right in one thing, mister. The Reverend McDowell's the man you should see. A reg'lar local historian.'

'You make me feel older than my years!'

Cannon said with a chuckle. 'But thank you kindly. I'll look up Mr McDowell, like you say. And I'm sorry about your stolen cows.'

They parted and Cannon walked away and swung up into his saddle on the patient steeldust. A light pressure of his knees, and under gathering storm clouds, he rode the gradient back onto the stage road, reviewing the encounter in his mind.

Running a small, family spread was a risky life in any times, and Cannon was not unfamiliar with it from his own boyhood circumstances ... before his father had finally dropped after working his guts out to make some city banker a profit on a crippling loan.

You slept when you could – which some seasons seemed like never – and you were always up before dawn in the same endless workaday grind, frequently to end up having Indians or rustlers or a goddamned drought turn all the striving to dust. You plunged deeper and deeper in debt in the desperate hope that *next* year would be the good one; the one that would let you break even.

Yes, he could surely sympathise with Dallas Perigo. His life, he sensed, would be an uphill battle. Cannon had seen the evidence of stock theft troubles himself, and with what sounded like a weak and ailing mother as well as a headstrong, not to mention disrespectful, younger brother, he'd have his hands more than full.

No wonder Perigo had looked a worried man.

3

The Powder-Keg Town

The icy rainwater trickled down inside the neck of Yale Cannon's yellow slicker and seeped up his sleeves. He didn't bend his head. He kept on riding, still outwardly the quiet, unmoved man with the carriage of a cavalry officer. But the lightning flickering over the foothills brought glints to his eyes, and the expression in the rugged face none was there to see told a different story.

He felt restless and strange.

The sensations came from deeper springs than the inconvenient opening of the skies. The discomforts of this storm would pass over fairly rapidly, if Cannon was any judge of the elements. He would then be able to resume the purposeful pace he'd been forced to slacken when his visibility became dangerously hindered by the heavy rain.

Yet besides the automatic caution the weather brought to bear on his riding, Cannon was preoccupied with the damnedest of niggles.

In his youth, he'd devoted his life to his country, believing in the Union and in his duty to use such dubious talents as he'd acquired to help it run. Now, with the years wearing on, and looking down his backtrail, he sensed something was missing.

In Antelope, he had the premonition, his life could be changed. But would it be for the better?

He pushed the unfamiliar, introspective sentiments to the back of his mind. In Antelope, he also had a fee to earn – a job he had hired on to do in his role as a federal marshal's deputy. Though he'd carefully refrained from mentioning it to the Perigos, this was what had to come first. For the present, he assured himself, the rest was just some conveniently truthful smokescreen. Period.

He was fixing that straight in his mind when the rain suddenly stopped and the clouds broke apart. The gloom lifted. The earth steamed under a slanting sun. Soon the colours of sunset lay red fire across the western rims.

He gigged the steeldust into an easy trot.

And so it was as he rode damply and quietly into the township of Antelope and made a brief tour of inspection.

Despite the rosy light of the westering sun,

it was a drab place, much as Cannon had been led to expect. A ranch town, and nothing more, where the inhabitants would scratch a living catering for the needs of the country's cattle bosses.

The layout evidenced a simple pattern of unplanned development by men anxious to get on quickly with the business of exploiting the frontier lands. A broad Main Street and several cross streets comprised a commercial heart, and outside that was a haphazard sprawl of dwellings, built to no particular style beyond the whim of the individual owners.

The buildings were mostly board and batten. Thrown up quickly, few of the walls had ever known paint. The wide planks had weathered to a stony grey under the harsh summer sun and scouring winter blizzards. The colour lent an atmosphere of antiquity and permanence Cannon recognized as illusory. These places sprang up like field mushrooms, and were often gone as quickly with a turn of their district's economic or social tide.

Merchants were shutting up shop on Main Street – the false-fronted general store, the bank, the harness shop, the gunsmith's, the town smithy. No one spoke to Cannon. Those who saw him sucked their teeth, and watched his passing silently. It was that kind of place, he thought – the kind where folks never missed a thing and a stranger or anything different from the norm was treated with suspicious reserve.

Men didn't ride in at this time, Cannon supposed; Antelope was preparing for a sleepy weeknight. Saturday and maybe Sunday would be the big days. Then the town would come to life as the playground for hard-working cowboys and cowmen from the fertile grazing lands that surrounded it. There might be horse racing, cockfighting and a general fandango at a large dance hall. On Sunday, Cannon imagined, the righteous would attend the neat, picket-fenced church, dressed in their best.

He splashed his way through Main

Street's rutted mud and puddles to the livery stable and turned his horse into the open runway beside the corral.

'I'd be obliged if you'd rub him down and give him some grain,' he told the old-timer who cared for the horses.

The hostler took one last suck at the short stem of a large, blackened and extinct corn-cob pipe, made a show of knocking it out and tucked it into his vest pocket. As the livery barn's dayman, he wasn't hankering for work at this hour, but in these parts jobs he could do would be hard come by at his time of life. He grunted.

'Fer a payin' customer, whatsoever yuh says, colonel.'

He used the address as another man would say mister, though given his client's military bearing, it might have sounded apt for once, even to his own ears.

'Thank you kindly,' Cannon said. He disregarded the hostler's absence of enthusiasm but shrewdly put his trust in a wage-earner's need to attend his employer's business.

They attended to the details in the harness room-cum-office. Then Cannon shouldered his saddlebags, caught up his rifle and returned on foot to the roadway.

The single hotel was situated on a corner at the other end of the street from the stone-built courthouse, jail and sheriff's office. It was the second most solid of the town's buildings; two storeys of brick with the pretentious legend Grand Union Hotel and the date 1875 standing out in masonry relief as part of the showy cornice above the upper windows.

The lobby was gloomy. It smelled, too – a compound of naphthalene and stale cooking odours and the early onset of decay.

The tinkling of a bell as Cannon let the street door swing shut on its patent spring hinges summoned the hotel keeper from an inner office to the polished rosewood counter beside the carpeted stairs. Cannon glimpsed a young woman seated on a stool at a high desk, poring over a ledger, in the moment the office door was open.

The landlord was a square, blocky, middle-aged man with iron-grey hair thinning on top, a rat-trap mouth and searching, yellow-balled eyes of the kind that didn't miss much.

'Five dollars a night, mister,' he told Cannon with a brusque, take-it-or-leave-it tone to his voice. 'Bath at the end of the hallway is thrown in. Meals are extra.'

Cannon checked in, signing his name on the register in bold, well-formed letters.

Up the faintly creaking stairs, the door of his room had a lock on it; the bed had springs; the linen looked clean. A washstand and commode offered basic facilities, including a fresh, folded towel. The floor was covered with a piece of well-trodden carpet. He hadn't been expecting more.

The hotel man raised a window. 'Staying long, Mr Cannon?'

'A day or two.'

'Business, huh? You a cattle buyer?'

'No. I have a personal matter to pursue, Mr – er–?'

'Brodie's the name. Jack Brodie.'

Cannon gave Brodie the same yarn he'd given the Perigos, didn't mention his clash with the brothers, but asked where he might find the Reverend McDowell.

Brodie was of a different breed to the young ranchers. His yellow eyes narrowed a mite, like he didn't entirely believe Cannon's story. No one suckered Jack Brodie.

'Parsonage'd be back o' the church, alongside the schoolhouse,' he clipped. 'You must of seen the church, Mr Cannon.'

'I believe I did, Mr Brodie.'

''Course, I could request young Miss Rose McDowell to show you over. Happens she's in my office downstairs right now ... helps with the book-keeping here. There's a power of the stuff, y'unnerstand. Howsumever I am paying her for the time.'

'Obliged,' Cannon said, taking the hint that Brodie would expect compensation. 'But it won't be necessary.'

Brodie spread his tree-trunk legs and stuck his hands in his pockets, thus revealing a

46

stretch of dingy vest adorned with a heavy gold watch chain. He went to speak, changed his mind, gave a curt nod, and shuffled out.

Cannon figured he was intrigued by his new guest. Overt prying was out, beyond the ostensibly casual questions he had already put and which had brought him inadequate satisfaction. In the West, a man's past history and motives were publicly acknowledged his own affairs.

Cannon wondered whether he had intended the McDowell girl to be a spy, witting or unwitting, as well as a guide. A shifty gent, his host. This Antelope was altogether a place of odd tensions, with its folks given over to suspicious reserve and furtive watchfulness.

There were towns a man rode into that he could tell by the feel of them were nice towns – self-respecting, at peace with themselves and the world. All things being equal, as largely they were, the citizenry of such places would be congenial. It came natural to be friendly and helpful.

But Antelope, he thought, was like a

powder-keg waiting for a spark. Why?

The wind had dropped to a whisper and the underbelly of a grey-blue strata of cook-fire smoke reflected the pools of lamplight that were the windows of the towners' dwellings. It was that time of evening when families gathered around tables and ate, not when strangers went calling.

Cannon stopped for a spell at a steamy-windowed restaurant and took care of his hunger. The meal was solid and palatable, but the fat lady who served it was unsmiling and uncommunicative.

He dined leisurely on a steak that was thick and juicy, vegetables that were not overcooked, and a big wedge of apple pie. He finished up with three cups of freshly made coffee, steaming and black.

'Thank you, ma'am. I do admire a good square meal. A man who has known hunger respects generous portions of well-prepared food.'

But the woman was indifferent to his compliment. She shrugged. 'Hereabouts you get given what you ask for.'

Cannon wondered just what those terse words were meant to signify, if anything. He was still studying on it when he skirted the church's picket fence, starkly white in the light of a rising moon, and saw lantern-light in the schoolhouse.

A young woman was inside, working with chalk and a will at a blackboard. She was engrossed in her work, but Cannon guessed she could not have seen him in the outer darkness even had she paused to look his way.

Cannon paused on the flower-edged walk that linked the schoolhouse to the darkened building looming ahead, which he assumed to be the parsonage. He watched.

The woman had unaffected grace and poise and wrote with sure, efficient strokes. This must be the redoubtable Miss Kate McDowell who, according to the Perigos, taught school and attended to a whole lot else in behalf of her ageing father. Preparing the next day's lessons, no doubt.

She wore a severe black dress, tidy but entirely devoid of trim. It was marked at the cuffs with chalk dust – and it failed to obscure an appealing femininity of which Cannon jumped to a conclusion she would herself be totally dismissive. Somehow, though he had never met her, he felt that he knew this young woman from someplace already.

She looked to be in her twenties and would have appeared more or less as she did now for something less than ten years. Cannon's memory for people and names was good and he knew that in this case it was playing him a trick, and Miss McDowell's familiarity was illusory, since a quick review of all the places he'd been in the past ten years failed to turn up a young lady who exuded such capability and assurance and whose appearance matched.

Suddenly, as though sixth sense alerted the schoolteacher to his presence, she stopped marking the blackboard and swiftly turned and walked toward the window. She stared directly, rolling the chalk thoughtfully in slim, sensitive fingers.

Cannon thought her eyes would be blue, but at this distance he could not know. She was mostly a womanly silhouette against the light behind her in the classroom. That she could see much of the dark outdoors through the glass was doubtful.

Yet on top of the slightly heady scent of flowers, an electricity charged the air. She was aware that she was watched. Maybe she had heard his footfalls on the walk, or possibly the small clink of a loose pebble as his boot kicked it aside.

Abruptly, she thrust open the casement. 'Who is that?' she said, boldly challenging the prowler he might be. 'Who's there?'

'Cannon's the name. Yale Cannon,' he said, lifting the pearl-coloured stetson. 'But it will signify nothing, Miss McDowell. I trust you would be the schoolteacher, the Reverend McDowell's eldest daughter?'

Now he had identified himself, the

anxious edge went from her voice, leaving it warm and pleasantly easy on the ear. 'You plainly have the advantage of me besides some honest purpose, Mr Cannon, and I bid you good evening. What brings you here?'

'I was hoping to speak with your father, ma'am.' He nodded toward the parsonage. 'But I see the house is in darkness, so I guess he must be out or already abed, in which case I shan't bother him.'

The girl looked puzzled, then laughed – not at him, and kindly. 'Oh, I see ... no lamps are lit.'

'That was what told me.'

'It told you wrong, I fear.' A note of regret crept into her voice. 'My father has little use for anything but the most powerful light these days, and that's God's own sun. Then he can read the large print in the church's big Bible, but not much else, and only with the help of strong spectacles.'

Cannon regarded her gravely. 'I'm sorry, ma'am. I had no idea...'

'That my father is near blind?' she completed forthrightly. 'As a stranger, there is no reason you should, nor any to apologize. Despite his failing sight, my father is always glad to receive visitors and do what he can to help his fellow man.'

She leaned out to pull the window to and Cannon couldn't help but notice she was strikingly built with a full bosom and a trim waist.

'Wait a minute,' she said, 'and I'll go with you up to the house.'

4

Jailbird

While Yale Cannon was making the acquaintance of the composed Miss Kate McDowell, at the other end of the sprawling main drag, Sheriff Willy Randers had at last found time to fossick through a pile of yellowing newspapers. These relics were kept – or allowed to moulder – on a window seat in the untidy room in the blocky stone courthouse building that was utilised as Antelope's law office.

Randers was a thick-set man getting along in years with a rounding paunch, close-cropped tow-coloured hair and a complexion that had never tanned – just reddened blotchily between patches of dry scaliness that seemed to spread inexorably with the advance of time.

His washed-out eyes recognized the paper he sought and he hauled it out with spatulate fingers. He grunted with satisfaction. It was a city rag, from faraway Tucson, Arizona, and all of three months old.

'Ain't nothin' wrong with your mem'ry, Willy ol' boy,' he told himself self-contentedly. 'Not that yuh need no newspaper fancifyin'. The facts an' his likeness is on the dodger plain enough.'

He lurched into the groaning swivel chair

behind the big deal table he used as a desk, put his boot heels on the gouged edge of its top and settled back to read.

Here was a nameless hack's spine-chilling account of the most recent and dastardly crime of one William 'Red' Effingham, lately of Yuma Penitentiary but one-time of Colorado.

'In a most remarkable instance of the audacity and insolence of the criminal class, William Effingham, a former convict, his sentence just recently completed, did effect an entrance at 2.30 a.m. into the residence in Tucson of Mr Howard Gamble, the much-esteemed merchant-tailor, and forcibly opened and purloined from the locked drawer of an escritoire a sum of money. How much money was stolen is not exactly known but it is conjectured the drawer contained between $40 and $50,' the paper said.

'The most tragic part of this affair was that the thief contrived to awaken the house in going clumsily about his burglarious business, and was confronted by Mr Gamble and his good wife. Then he did take out a pistol and point-blank and in cold blood shoot the householder dead...'

Randers lowered the paper and tutted with a ponderous shake of his head. He scanned through the rest of the breathlessly written piece – which expanded upon the opening sentences with much lurid and sensational detail – and dwelled with satisfaction on the last paragraph which re-informed him that the estate of the late Mr Gamble was offering a reward of $1000 to whosoever was instrumental in bringing the killer to justice.

Sheriff Randers was musing dreamily on what a thousand-dollar roll of greenbacks might look like, and on how men could spend it, when a harsh voice shouted him out of his dreams.

'Hey, tinbadge! Come on in here! I want to talk.'

The back of Randers' thick neck reddened. His prisoner's tone got right up his nose. It went with the cocky confidence he'd exhibited ever since he'd first hauled him in and locked him up in the Antelope calaboose.

Randers got up and stumped to the wide-open inner doorway that gave entrance to the jailhouse.

'Shut your trap, jailbird. It's high time you 'preciated this is a deep hole you've fallen into, showin' your face in a decent folks' town.'

Having got the sheriff's attention the prisoner rolled off his cot and spat contemptuously in the direction of the slops pail in the corner of his iron cage, which was the nearest to the door. He came up to the bars, closing bony hands around them.

He threw stringy red hair off his face with a toss of his head and sneered. 'Reckon you don't know the half of it, Mister Smart-ass Sheriff. There's a lot I c'd tell you about your decent town if'n I had a mind to.'

Randers bottled up his anger, eyes bulging, massive jaw clenched. He wasn't going to let this runty outlaw bait him.

The moment he'd first sighted him in the saloon he knew Effingham, though well into his middle years, thought he was a real hotshot the way he carried himself, tied-down guns and all. Well, he was no longer gun-hung, but he still had the lean, predatory look of a vicious killer with eyes like cold, muddy creek water. And his arrogance stuck in Randers' craw.

The sheriff tried to match his prisoner's sneer with one of his own.

'The way you're gettin' on, jailbird, sounds like you reck'n you should be the gent roddin' the law in this bailiwick.'

He laughed at this cumbrous repartee and pulled his makings from his vest pocket.

'I guess I been *ast,* near enough,' Effingham said.

Randers tried not to let his surprise show, but the wheatstraw paper in his left hand shook and several flakes of the Bull Durham he shook from its muslin sack drifted to the floor.

'You've been asked?' he said thickly.

'That's what I said, didn't I?'

'The hell you did!' Randers growled. 'What kinda bullshit is that?'

'Jest the honest truth, badge-toter.' Effingham grinned. 'The low-down is, the cow nurses are gettin' plenty sick o' the rustlin' a-goin' on in your precious bailiwick, Randers. They sees a gun-handy gent like my own self, it stands to reason they sound him out. Mebbe we c'd do a deal.'

Randers goggled. 'A deal?'

'Sure. You turn a blind eye an' let me outa here. Then I pay back with what they offer me to clean those pesky Pryorites offa the mesa an' outa their hair.'

Randers was mightily affronted. 'That's bribery an' corruption of a lawfully elected peace officer, mister,' he growled, keeping his anger by dint of a self-control he hadn't known he had.

He scowled and gulped. ''Sides, the town's got a thousand dollars ridin' on turnin' you in to the federal marshals.'

Effingham scoffed. 'A thousand dollars! That's chickenfeed, Sheriff. Ain't no more'n one fifth o' what the State of Missouri offered for ol' Jesse and Frank.'

Randers overlooked Effingham's swaggering attempt to put himself in the same class as the murderous, train-robbing James brothers. He said, 'It sure beats a cut o' what Antelope's cattlemen can pay you for houndin' damnfool religious folks up on their Jerusalem Pastures. An' who says them's the wideloopers?'

'They says, so we don't pay no never mind to nothin' else. An' I got another score to settle with this Abel Anson Pryor anyhow.' Effingham dropped his voice to a confidential level. 'Moreover, once he's a-strummin' a harp up yonder, the way's gonna be clear fer me to be a rich man, Sheriff. If you was wise, you'd play along an' be my pard–'

'Aw! Hush your yap, willya?' Randers interrupted him, his voice rising to a bellow. 'I ain't listenin' to no more o' your poppycock, Effingham! No gallows-bait makes a fool o' me. You're goin' back to Arizona to stand trial for murder.'

With that Randers swung around and stumped back into his office, slamming the heavy door shut behind him.

But the ex-convict fascinated him all the same and it was not as easy to close his mind like he had the door.

Earlier, when challenged about the crime in Tucson, Effingham had tried to feed him some cock-and-bull story about the tailor trying to disarm him and the gun going off accidentally.

He'd also told him he'd only needed the $30 he stole to get him back to Antelope. It was the stamping ground of his youth before the War Between the States, he'd said, as though this were a motive that made theft and killing justifiable

Whatever the facts of the matter, Effingham's previous sojourn had pre-dated Randers' tenure here. Probably he'd been part of the gold rush crowd in the years before the mines up at High Crossing had played out.

That in itself was a puzzle for Randers.

What now would bring a one-time miner of Effingham's stripe back here? Idle talk had it he'd been a Southern sympathizer during the war, then unreconstructed bank robber and road agent after. Ten years in the harsh Yuma Penitentiary had plainly failed to reform him.

Effingham was scarcely the sentimental type, doing things for old time's sake. Most likely he'd be of the tumbleweed inclination: a drifter who'd wander all over, just seeing the sights, shying off honest work, never staying long in one place.

Yet on his own declaration he had come to Antelope with a purpose – killed to put the coin in his pockets to make the very journey, he claimed.

What was that purpose?

Sheriff Randers was also more than a mite concerned by Effingham's revelation that the country's ranching interests were minded to take the law into their own hands.

'My oath, I'll be a g'damn' Cheyenne buck if I let that happen!' he swore.

Yale Cannon saw the Reverend Ephraim McDowell sitting alone in a massive oak-framed chair in the chimney corner in the darkness of the parsonage's front parlour. The flickering of a pine-log fire etched the deep lines of his ageing face and was reflected in the thick lenses of the heavy pair of spectacles that masked his eyes.

'We have a visitor, papa,' Kate announced at the parlour door, ahead of Cannon. She went in directly and put a match to the wick of one of the lamps in the mantelshelf brackets. 'You can come on in, Mr Cannon.'

Mr McDowell pulled out a second pair of glasses from a pocket in the folds of an enveloping gown and put them on over the top of the pair he already wore.

'Cannon,' he mused. 'Who are you, sir? I do believe I've never had the pleasure...'

'That's correct, Mr McDowell,' Cannon said. 'This is the first time I've travelled to your town, though it's something I've been minded to do from way back. You could call me a private gentleman in search of a piece of his past.'

In the spell it had taken Cannon to complete the walk to the parsonage with the minister's daughter, what he'd been told by the Perigo brothers had taken on a new complexion.

If Dallas Perigo had sounded rawly jealous about Kate's activities in behalf of her father, it was now understandable. A dim-sighted father would take up a whole load of a dutiful daughter's time and energy. No doubt she would have to shoulder many of the important responsibilities the minister bore to his congregation. This would come on top of the demands of teaching school. Where could Dallas fit in?

And the bratty Mel's soured-up resentment of her was also explained, Cannon thought. A watchful Kate would probably be acting as her father's parental eyes where her younger sister, Rose, was concerned.

The ridges across Mr McDowell's brow deepened. 'A piece of your past – here?' he asked Cannon.

'Surely, Mr McDowell. Like I said, I've never been in this country before, but I understand old friends of mine moved in many years back. I – uh – lost touch, but it would do my heart good to know what became of them. They were settlers; a family by the name of Bell.'

Cannon could not be sure, but the old minister's stiffness seemed suddenly to become something more than the characteristic of advancing years.

In a brittle voice, he said, 'Might your yearning not be a vanity, Mr Cannon? The Good Book warns us against treasures on earth, where moth and rust doth corrupt and where thieves break through and steal. Lay up your treasures in heaven; there will your heart be also.'

Cannon bowed to the preacher's words. 'I'm a plain man, minister – just an ex-soldier – and lack your scholarly grasp of the

Scriptures' messages. However, it was intimated that as the town's longest surviving inhabitant, your knowledge of local history could help me.'

Mr McDowell opened his mouth as though to reply, then he appeared to bite back the words and he shook his head. After a pause, he said, 'Stranger, whoever told you that has led you off the true paths. I must remember to make clear from the pulpit the futility and waywardness of dwelling in the past.' He warmed to the theme and added more strongly, 'Forgive, repent and look forward to the kingdom of God.'

It was difficult for Cannon to assess the cleric's mood. The thick glasses obscured his eyes, in which Cannon might have read more.

'I'm disappointed you can give no more particular guidance, sir.'

Kate had been following the exchange attentively, looking on her parent with tender affection, and now tried to explain away his crustiness.

'My father's memories are not all pleasant, Mr Cannon. I'm sure that as a former military man you wouldn't contest that where old wars are concerned there are things best left forgotten. We have today's devils to fight.'

'Well put, my dear,' McDowell said. 'Why stir up what the years have laid to rest when God's urgent mission for us here is to save Antelope from a false messiah?'

Cannon frowned his puzzlement. He tried to fit in the odd twists of this conversation with what he'd already heard from the Perigo brothers – the hints of counter-atrocities in the wake of the Sand Creek Massacre, the Pryorite newcomers on the mesa whom they accused of stealing their beef – and the brooding atmosphere he'd experienced in passing through the town. He sighed raggedly.

'You folks must speak as you think best, I guess...'

Kate seemed to divine the cause of his frustration. 'You don't know much about our local circumstances, do you, Mr Cannon?'

'Not a whole lot,' he admitted. 'It would be a great favour, ma'am, if you were kindly to enlighten me what it is that troubles this town.'

Kate looked to her father and Cannon saw a barely perceptible nod.

'The thorn in our flesh is one Abel Anson Pryor,' she began.

'I've heard the name. Isn't he a man of the cloth, like the Reverend McDowell?'

McDowell stirred like a dog irritated by a flea and growled under his breath, 'A very different cloth!'

'Brother Pryor is the founder and leader- of a religious sect,' said Kate. 'He and his converts have established a community on a high mesa situated back of the ghost gold-mining town of High Crossing, upriver from Antelope. The settlers farm to sustain themselves, their families and Pryor's church. They've renamed their meadows Jerusalem Pastures.'

Mr McDowell exploded angrily. 'Bah! Call it Doomsday Mesa, young woman! True believers do!'

Kate ignored the outburst. 'Mr Pryor has unorthodox teachings, Mr Cannon, of which no right-thinking person should approve, but he has a commanding presence and a powerful talent for oratory. It makes father angry to see the nesters come in droves, foolishly drawn by his magnetism. They're poorly educated, Eastern folk for the most part, gullible or willing to be lured by the false promises of a bountiful life. And the country's ranchers suspect the people of the mesa rustle their cattle – also fear they will tamper with the watercourses that keep their spreads below green and fertile.'

At last Cannon began to get an inkling of what it was that kept the cow-town on edge and resentful of newcomers. What was not explained to his entire satisfaction was the personal hostility of Kate's father. Cannon was not a fanciful man, yet he felt it oppressively, like a looming storm.

Mr McDowell's voice was acid. 'So you

see, Mr Cannon, this is no pretty scene, and the people you are looking for are not on it. Therefore it would be best if you rode on.'

Cannon suspicioned that had he been a line rider begging for jobs or alms, shabbily clothed and toting a bedroll and a worn saddle as all his worldly goods, he might have gotten a more neutral reception.

As it was, he received the clear impression that a younger and fitter Ephraim McDowell would have just upped and kicked his tail right off the place.

5

Rose

Jack Brodie came back into the Grand Union Hotel's lobby. In the office at the rear, Rose McDowell looked up from the ledger in which she was making entries from a stack of accounts and watched him study the new name in the register, narrowing his yellowed eyes. He frowned and scratched his balding scalp.

'Cannon, huh? He's gone to your pa's, Rose. What's he after in Antelope, I ask.'

'Did he not say?'

'Yeah. Some sort of rigmarole about running down folks he knowed once living hereabouts – lest I mistook him.'

Brodie added the rider with a sarcastic sneer, borne out by his next observation. 'I got a feeling about this jasper. Mebbe he was lying an' mebbe not, but it's my guess there's more'n he's telling.'

'Guessing never got anybody anywhere,' Rose said prettily. She toyed contemplatively with her raven hair. This was a habit she had developed till it was near instinctive and which she culminated by pushing a hand up under the dark tresses while she tossed her head a little to shake them out and let them fall again. It was an artful gesture and one she was aware menfolk found charming.

In truth, Rose had little time for the hotel landlord and his suspicious mind. But she could ill-afford to displease him. Rose's ambition at age seventeen was to rule her own life. She longed to shake off the dust of this ramshackle cow-town and its – to her – dreary environs.

However, she was not naïve, Rose assured herself. To flee to and flower in the brighter sunshine of California with her beau, she needed money. The clerk's work put her way by Jack Brodie was the means to build up a stake.

How she resented her dogmatic, severely Puritan father and her smart-alec sister! She was a grown woman now, not a school-kid. The changes were there for all to see. The coltish lines of adolescence had all disappeared and the contours of her lovely body were gratifyingly feminine, even though at her kinsfolk's leading they were contained by drab grey homespun stuff when she would have preferred colourful cotton print of the kind her father considered vulgar.

Why wouldn't they treat her and Mel as the woman and the man they were and let them marry? Mel had sworn that when they had enough money, they would elope.

'Sure,' Brodie went on, pursuing the subject in hand. 'Guessing ain't nowhere near good enough. I savvy that. What game is he playing, this Mr Cannon – if that really is his name?'

Rose shrugged. 'What's it got to do with anybody?' she asked, a mite recklessly.

'Simply this,' Brodie snapped. 'We got to keep our eyes peeled. Things are ticklish around Antelope. The rancher crowd is raising hell over them thieving mesa folk, and that jackass Randers ain't done nothing bar lock up a gun-handy looking gent who was raring to clean out the whole nest of 'em.'

Rose bristled but kept her feelings from showing. 'There's no proof any of Mr Pryor's settlers are rustlers,' she said evenly.

'Careful now, Rose. This here burg depends on the cattle trade an' it'll go bad with us to speak ag'inst the rancher interests.

With those religion-crazy Pryorites roaming onto the free graze and setting on the water, anything's likely to happen, most any time. Why, they're dangerous – what's the word? – *heretics*. Your pa, a real man o' God, says that!'

Rose bit her tongue. Much of her father's opposition to Brother Abel Anson Pryor was in her opinion due to jealousy of his charisma and his ever-growing following. Kate scoffed and said she was young and impressionable, but Rose found herself very attracted by Pryor's powerful preaching and showmanship. His brand of religion was so unlike her father's. It was all-encompassing, stirring. For certain, the Reverend McDowell's congregation could not match Pryor's adherents in number or commitment.

The unacceptability of Pryor's community to the ranchers and their conventional town also appealed to the mischief-maker in Rose.

'Do you think Mr Cannon has connections with the Pryorites, Mr Brodie?' Doubt was in Rose's voice as she pictured the soldierly new guest.

'Naw, not exactly ... though I reckon if there's any link-up we should find out about it and – uh – post our fellow citizens.'

'What is it you're suggesting?'

'Well, I figure it's our duty to take a little look-see while he's out. Never know just who a stranger might be, what he might be carrying in amongst his belongings.

Rose caught Brodie's drift clearly enough. The high-handed hotel man wanted to pry but being the hypocrite he was, he had to justify it. Moreover, he was too yellow to run the risk of being caught rummaging himself.

Actually, she thought such sneakiness by a host was contemptible and showed no respect for a guest's rights. Yet she was not pure-minded enough to make her dislike active. Nor to fall out with her part-time employer. Nor to miss the chance of reward. She took the initiative.

'Do you propose this look-see is a job for me?'

'You read my thoughts exactly, girl,' Brodie said. 'It would be far better that way. I got to stay at the desk, to delay Mr Cannon in case he should return sudden.'

'Of course. Well, I guess I could be encouraged...'

'Sure, a five-dollar bonus sounds appropriate to me, and mebbe others would be strong for paying more – depending on what we find, of course.'

The temptation was beyond refusal. It was an easy assignment; the risk of being surprised, slim. And Rose was mindful of the ever-imminent showdown that could occur at the parsonage between herself and her father and sister, while at the Crazy-P relationships between Mel and his bossy brother were likewise strained. If the persecuted pair were forced to run out on it all, they'd be right glad of every extra dollar.

Rose took the key Brodie gave her and slid away on her assignment, up the creaking stairs to the room where Yale Cannon and his bags had been accommodated.

She opened the largest of the bags and poked through it, taking care to leave everything as she found it – clean socks, a clean shirt, a handsome blue bandana, handkerchiefs, longjohns...

The tally was not promising, so she turned to the other bag, a kind of buckskin satchel which she had saved for second and last, as though in unconscious expectation it would prove the more revealing.

It yielded several cardboard boxes of gun cartridges, a small can of oil and a chamois, a claspknife, a leather-and-brass telescope, tobacco in a muslin sack, a three-week-old Arizona newspaper, a Bible, then, beneath that, another glint of metal and wrapped in oiled silk, some folded papers.

Rose eased these last items out from under the calf-bound black book. Handling the Bible with trembling fingers brought upon her a late twinge of conscience which she fought down.

The glinting metal was a badge. She noted its inscription before turning to the thick papers that crackled as she laid them out flat on the bed.

An official red seal and imposing signatures reiterated the story told by the badge. She did not have to read many lines to ascertain they were papers of commission issued to a field deputy of a United States Federal Marshal appointed directly by the President. Yale Cannon was appointed and empowered to execute all orders and processes of the courts.

There was also a letter, and to this she did give powerful pause. Then she rewrapped the papers in their oilskin and hurriedly restored each item to the position in which she had found it in the satchel. Jack Brodie was beside himself when he heard what she had learned. 'I knew it sure as shooting – an undercover lawdog!' he exclaimed smugly. 'And come here to escort that gunfighter pilgrim back to the scene of his alleged crimes! It sticks in my craw to think of old Randers fixing to bolster his reputation. Writ a letter, did he? Well, that beats all, but

I ain't surprised.'

A petulant frown marred Rose's smooth white brow. 'What do you mean? Surely Sheriff Randers is only doing his duty? This Red Effingham is a criminal and a dangerous ruffian.'

Brodie shook his head sadly and wisely. 'I shouldn't let the cow-men hear you say that, Rose. It's Effingham's hardcase talents they was counting on to put a fear greater than God inta Pryor and his hymn-singing hoe-men!'

'Why, that's despicable!'

Brodie was cynical. 'The way of the world, young lady.'

'Well, I'm pleased Sheriff Randers knows what's right and is doing it.'

If it came to fighting trouble between the Pryorites and a terrorizing band of the district's ranchers misguidedly assisted by a murderous miscreant, Rose knew on whose side of the fence her sympathies would lie.

Brodie clucked his tongue inside his rat-trap mouth. 'It's thinking like your'n that'd ruin this town. This is a *cow*-town, girl, an' long-term it don't pay none of us citizens to forget it. We got to think of our livelihoods, y'see?'

'How horrible! I'm certain Mr Randers and the marshal's deputy will have no truck with such unprincipled ideas.'

Brodie gave a nasty bark of a laugh. 'The highly esteemed Mr Randers might be in for a shock. The stockmen've already said he's a town marshal more'n he's a sheriff. He looks after his town a whole lot better'n the rest of his bailiwick. And like I says, that ain't even in the towners' best interest.'

With this, Brodie clammed up on his subversive hints, as though he recognized he might have said too much.

Rose's head swam. Her loyalties, such as they might be, were more confused than ever, but amidst the consideration of local jealousies, rivalries and politics, self-interest remained dominant.

After quick thought, she said into the silence, 'We will be careful to let no one know that we've discovered Mr Cannon's secret, won't we? Heaven knows what the consequences might be if it was gossiped that we'd searched his rig!'

Brodie chuckled. 'Don't you fuss your pretty little head, Rose. Your part is just between you and me, huh? What happens now will be men's business. An' tonight's meeting of the law and order committee is a plumb convenient starting place.'

But Rose worried anyhow.

What lay behind Yale Cannon's masquerade as a man on a sentimental journey? And why was he visiting her father?

The only aspect of her findings that comforted her was the promise of Red Effingham's transportation real soon to distant Tucson, Arizona.

The 'men's business' to which Jack Brodie alluded did not exclude Kate McDowell. Civic affairs in Antelope seldom did. Later that same evening found a select gathering convened in a private back room of the Four

Aces Saloon adjacent to the Grand Union Hotel – some dozen men in all, prominent ranchers and the towners who served them. Plus Kate.

Kate McDowell had somehow gotten herself appointed this *ad hoc* committee's secretary. She had never quite figured how, but knew it had a lot to do with her ability to keep minutes, and maybe a little besides with the flattering ambitions manifestly entertained by the handsome young owner of the Crazy-P.

Dallas Perigo made a poor fist of disguising the fact that he was much taken with her and held her in the highest regard. But Dallas was well thought of by his peers and many of the district's elders. They had fallen in line with his suggestion that the committee should avail itself of her capabilities.

Not exactly to a man, however.

Some resented her and held that she was 'uppish'. Kate thought they perhaps feared they'd met their match in wits that were daily challenged and sharpened by the fresh, untamed spirit in her schoolroom charges.

Jack Brodie was one who neither appreciated her talents nor recognized that times were a-changing. He abhorred her 'suffragist notions', Dallas had confided to her.

Well, that was just too bad. It was high time the women of the West had an improved lot. Kate saw the ranch wives, weathered to coarseness by the elements, worn out and aged before their time by constant work and child-bearing. She saw these women and pitied them, and would strive in any cause that might better their lives, regardless of the hidebound opinions of a hundred Jack Brodies.

It was Brodie who was holding forth this moment. 'Yeah, it's more'n that damnfool Randers horning in now, gents. This jasper's booked in at the hotel and I just so happens to l'arn he's a sticky-billed marshal's deppity all the ways from Arizona...' He paused significantly on the name of the territory. 'Like our friend Effingham that Randers has slammed in the hoosegow.'

'Is Mr Effingham our *friend*, Mr Brodie?' Kate probed with quiet purpose.

It did not take much to stoke Brodie's enmity from coolness to heat. His gaze darkened.

'Sure, Miss Kate! Ever'body on this committee knowed he was just the thing – the one that could turn the card against cussed Pryor an' his bunch of thieves!'

Kate calmly flicked back through the pages of her minutes book. 'I don't think "everybody" is quite correct. The motion to enlist Mr Efflngham's help was not carried unanimously.'

'Aw! Near enough! You're splitting hairs, ma'am! What I said about Effingham goes as it lays anyhow. He was a two-gun toter an' he oughta be purty good with 'em.'

Kate noticed that Dallas Perigo's troubled frown had been deepening with every word of the exchange between herself and the hotel-keeper. She opened her mouth to make another tart retort – and he cut across her with unusual rudeness.

'What is it you're fixin' to say, Jack Brodie?'

'I figure we're all cow-men here or depend on the cattle trade's business. We sorta scratch each other's backs, so it'd make a whole lotta sense if we was to look at a certain bright idea that occurs to me.'

'A bright idea?' Dallas said tautly. 'What is it?'

'That we move in ahead o' this hood-winking lawman, afore he shows his colours an' whiles we got just that stumbling fool Randers to see about.'

'I don't get your drift...'

Brodie gave a brittle laugh that had neither humour nor warmth in it. 'Why, boy, we move in an' spring Red Effingham outa jail!'

6

Gunfire!

Dallas Perigo was dumbstruck. An excited buzz ran around the rest of the company. Only Kate was ready with a swift reply.

'Mr Brodie, you forget yourself. This is a law and order committee.'

Brodie scoffed. 'We called it that, for sure, but I reckon a school ma'am is smart enough to of knowed it was set up more prexactly on account o' the Pryorite skunks.'

Sitting beside Dallas, Mel Perigo chewed his lip. For once, Kate thought, the brash youngster looked almost as worried as his silent brother, to whom she now looked for support.

Dallas shuffled his boots and growled to the room at large, 'I guess some did speak to

Effingham, but that was afore Sheriff Randers ran him in. Mebbe we should put this idea of Mr Brodie's to the vote.'

This met with a murmur of approval.

Dallas said, 'Remember, friends, Willy Randers has gotten a big followin' in town, specially among the womenfolk. Some reckon he does pretty well as sheriff.'

'Course they do,' said Brodie placatingly. 'But we can fix things so's we don't actually have to tread on his corns. I ain't proposing we go off half-cocked... We'll nat'rally go careful, be sorta clever, y'unnerstand?'

He addressed the last to Dallas like he was talking to an idiot and his hard mouth curled into a cold, contemptuous smile.

The meeting gave Kate the impression it was pleased to accept the balm Brodie was offering for its twinging consciences. Nor did it much care for being considered lacking in intelligence.

'Hear, hear,' somebody murmured, and the words were taken up around the room.

Dallas frowned. 'I don't know that I can

87

ride along with them there sentiments. The Pryorites need somebody to put an outsize boot inta their shenanigans an' keep 'em offa our graze. But if'n yuh suggestin' we should go actin' behind a good man's back and likely do somethin' hotheaded an' foolish–'

'Aw, the hell with it!' Brodie interjected. 'The question is, do we want Effingham out an' gunning for us or not. Let's quit the goddamn bellyaching!'

'There's a lady present, Mr Brodie.'

Kate shrewdly suspected that Dallas, though he might be truly caring of her sensitivities, also appreciated her strengths and knew it took more than blasphemous language to shock her. She did not envy his position; divided feelings would be un-avoidable for him. Yet he needed to object, so these were the easier grounds he chose.

'Why so there is, Mr Perigo,' Brodie said, his voice oily with sarcasm. 'My apologies, ma'am.'

Kate dipped her head but refused to meet Brodie's eye.

He sucked in a deep breath. 'Now then, gents, can we stop messing?' A crafty smile came to the heavy-jowled face. 'A vote was what Mr Perigo suggested, I believe... Well, how about we put it to one right now?'

Kate saw that Dallas' tactic was about to blow up in his face. When hands were shown, only one was raised in dissent – Kate's own – while Dallas and his brother abstained.

Kate was disappointed, yet she also felt deeply for Dallas. He was red-faced and uncomfortable, clearly torn between his affection for her and a hatred of the Pryorite menace which was his common tie with the rest of the ranching community.

Even Mel, whom Kate had hardly considered strong in moral judgment, looked put out by the near unanimous vote.

'Well, seems like we'll do anythin' to get the edge on the mesa preacher-man,' Mel grumbled under his breath. 'We're runnin' a risk. Red Effingham is a gunhawk an' don't belong on this range no more'n the Pryorite crowd.'

Brodie, mightily pleased with himself and anticipating glory and profit as the saviour of Antelope, strained his vest with his puffed-up chest and snorted.

'Yea, verily,' he said. 'But we don't need no cub puncher to tell us nothing about that. Soon as Effingham's scared the hypocritical clodhoppers out, we'll stop backing his play an' pay 'im off. I know his stripe. He ain't got nothing to stick around for. Why, he'll be gone before you can say Jack Robinson.'

Mel folded his arms in what Kate took to be sulky silence. Maybe he sensed that in opposing the prevailing mood while Dallas pulled in, he had gone to his tether.

Kate was slightly surprised he'd advanced his opinion at all in such company. Still, it was in keeping with his juvenile arrogance. Unlike his elder brother, Mel had always lacked in natural modesty and a proper sense of the fitness of things.

But she wondered if the youngster could like herself see the potential ugliness in the building, vigilante-type situation.

She scratched away rapidly in the minutes book, aghast at what she was recording but seemingly helpless to avert it.

After he'd left the minister and his daughter at the parsonage, Yale Cannon returned to his room at the Grand Union Hotel. He'd ridden several long days on the trail and he wisely planned some quiet reading, then a night's restorative shuteye between crisp sheets in a genuine bed.

Tomorrow morning would be plenty early enough to declare himself to the sheriff of Antelope, he determined.

Cannon frowned when he went to his smaller buckskin bag. He was unable to figure exactly why, but he could have sworn his personal belongings were not how he would have packed them himself.

A chill traced itself along his spine. Had someone tried to pilfer his stuff?

No, the door to his room had been locked like he'd left it, there was no sign it having been forced, and a fast check told him nothing was missing. He was getting foolish, a mite crazy maybe. 'It can happen when a hombre grows too accustomed to being on his lonesome,' he warned himself.

But there was another thing. The faintest suggestion of a floral scent hung in the air. It had not been there before, Cannon was sure, and no flowers were in the room. Lavender-water – that was what it was, he suddenly decided.

Yet if it were, that, too, presented a small, niggling mystery. Somehow these matters served to remind him of the oddness of the welcome he'd gotten from the Reverend McDowell.

Welcome? It had been purely the reverse!

Cannon found during the next couple of hours that he could not relax. Neither the stale events in his Arizona newspaper nor the comfort of favoured passages in his much-worn Bible would hold his wandering attention. And he was wide awake with nerve ends inexplicably tingling.

His own restlessness was beginning to irk

him and he was bunching his jaw grimly when a light tap came at the door.

'What is it?' he snapped. Only a disinterested night clerk had seen him come back to the hotel earlier. The man had been dozing in a chair behind the lobby counter and had barely acknowledged his mannerly 'good night'.

To his astonishment, a woman's voice answered in low, urgent tones. 'Mr Cannon! I have something important to tell you.'

Cannon thought he recognized the voice and was puzzled. 'Is that Miss Kate McDowell?' He rose to his feet and with a swift, cat-like tread started for the door.

'Correct, Mr Cannon. Will you please see me?'

Cannon moved to one side of the door and flattened himself against the wall.

He had no fear of a lone woman. Leastways, not of Kate McDowell, who had struck him as being in every respect a most admirable lady. But the oppressive broodiness of Antelope spooked a man and training and experience had made wariness a habit.

His right hand hovered toward the gun under his left armpit. With his left he reached over and yanked open the door.

To his reassurance Kate McDowell was indeed alone, which in itself heaped yet another riddle at his feet. Well-bred young women did not come furtively and un-accompanied to the hotel rooms of men of new and slight acquaintance.

'Please enter, ma'am. I can't think what compels you to come calling at this late hour, but my ear's all yours.'

Cannon stepped back into the room. Kate came in and herself closed the door softly behind her and leaned her back and the palms of her hands on it. She sighed as though relieved her coming had attracted no pursuing attention.

'You must forgive my intrusion, Mr Cannon, but I am at my wits' end for some-one to turn to.'

Cannon bowed his head with solemn

gentility. 'Then I am honoured, ma'am.'

'From what I've learned this past hour, it seemed you were the right person and there was no time to lose.' Before Cannon could reply with a modest dismissal, she forthrightly rushed on. 'Mr Cannon, it's true, isn't it, that despite what you told my father you're a deputy federal marshal come here to execute a warrant against the sheriff's prisoner, Effingham?'

The bat of an eyelid betrayed Cannon's surprise. 'It is,' he said. 'But nonetheless for that my inquiries of your father were genuine. Who besides yourself should think otherwise?'

He delivered the confirmation and the question in the same steady voice, masking his annoyance.

'By now I fear much of the town must be aware of your true identity, Mr Cannon. It was announced at a meeting of a small but influential committee we have to safeguard our interests against those of Mr Pryor's sometimes militant settlers.'

'I see,' said Cannon, though there was much he did not. 'And you've been delegated to tell me this?'

'No! I come in my own behalf and speak confidentially, Mr Cannon. The night clerk was fortunately snoring, so I was able to take the liberty of consulting the register for your room number and tiptoed past. No one knows I'm here.'

Cannon's smile was grim. 'A *secret* errand, Miss McDowell. Plainly you have a purpose yet to be revealed.'

Kate nodded. 'I'm afraid I see it as my duty to inform you that certain of the high-handed inhabitants hereabouts have decided the fugitive Effingham has talents that can be put to good use in running off Mr Pryor's community.'

Cannon stifled a gasp of anger. 'I'm sorry to hear this, ma'am.'

'Mr Cannon, I feel deeply guilty about this. Is it right of me to ask you to intervene – possibly endanger your very life – to save others from the consequences of their own monstrous folly?'

'Miss McDowell, I've taken an oath to uphold the authority of the American courts.'

'Then I plead with you to show your hand and deter my misguided compatriots from executing their earnest intention.'

'Which is...?'

'To release Effingham from jail this very night!'

Cannon remained rigid; his reaction was dry.

'By thunder, they do mean to steal a march on me, don't they? What are the odds? Surely there must be some who are sticklers for justice and sanity?'

'Sheriff Anders and his deputies, of course, but of the cattlemen and the towners, precious few – except perhaps the Perigos, whom I believe you've met.'

Cannon saw the suspicion of a blush colour Kate's even features, but he refrained from comment, and she felt compelled to uplift her beautiful but worried face to him and go on.

'Dallas has suffered stock losses as great as anyone's and his land runs right up to Jerusalem Pastures. He is open and generous, I believe, but he has been worn down by the struggle to make a living from the Crazy-P. He and his brother were left the property by their father's untimely death five years ago. His mother is a frail, dependent woman, and Mel stays a child – shiftless and cocky and unaware of his own ignorance.'

Cannon agreed. 'So I've seen, and maybe it's no wonder without a father around in his formative years – and I don't doubt his brother is too burdened to lick him into shape.'

'Yet it was Mel who did the objecting after the meeting carried the proposal concerning Effingham.' Kate spoke musingly, almost to herself, as though this aspect came back to her with renewed surprise.

'Hmm! So in fact Mr Dallas Perigo sits on the fence, I take it.'

Kate sighed and clenched her hands together in front of her breasts. 'Well ... yes, that would be true,' she seemed shamed into admitting. 'But it's my conviction there's very strong excuse for the division of his loyalties.'

Cannon raised his hands, open-palmed. 'I intended no criticism, ma'am,' he drawled. 'Forgive me for wanting to assess the matter bluntly. I see considerable trouble brewing. There may be violence, some death, and it would be wise to know on what numbers I can count... Few, I take it.'

Kate's control seemed finally to snap in an outburst of exasperation. 'Oh, I wish we were in someplace other than Antelope! Anywhere in the whole wide world! If I had the chance, I'd pack my bags and leave tomorrow!'

Cannon disputed it with a shake of his head and laid a fatherly hand on her shoulder.

'No, you would not, young woman,' he said gravely. 'You have your father and your school, and commitments it's beyond you to shirk.'

99

Kate mastered her feelings and lifted her chin to match his own drill-straight gaze. 'No, you're right – I cannot run away from it. Anyway, it's really my sister Rose who foolishly thinks the rest of the world is full of fun and freedom.'

'And it's not.'

'I'm well-read, Mr Cannon. I'm perfectly aware that it's full instead of fighting and grief. We as simple individuals will never put a stop to that. But we can stand by what we think is right and trust our faith will prevail, though it takes a thousand years.'

'I could not have put it–'

All at once, he was interrupted by a rapid exchange of gunfire ... followed by the shouts of men and the screams of women.

'Gunplay, Mr Cannon! They must be attacking the jailhouse already!'

Cannon rushed to the window, taking care to keep to its side in case of stray shots.

'No, ma'am. Much closer than that. A fight in the place next door – the Four Aces Saloon, I believe.'

7

Four Aces Rough-House

'I tell yuh, Rose, hell is gonna break loose round here! Thar'll be crazy men rarin' to butcher each other. Effingham's their ace of spades!'

Mel Perigo had given his distracted brother the slip and sneaked along to the parsonage where he had drawn Rose McDowell's attention by the practised expedient of tossing gravel at her upper storey bedroom window. Now they were together in the dimly moonlit buggy shed at the rear of the parsonage where they customarily kept their illicit trysts.

The young rancher was put out – more greatly worried than he'd dared let on at the committee meeting. His brother's quandary over the decision to free Red Effingham sprang from a system of values Mel didn't share, even held in contempt. But Mel, egged along by Rose, also had his own irons in the smouldering fire.

A groan came from Rose's pretty throat as her suitor finished pouring out his tidings of the committee's meeting.

'Oh, Mel! I wish I'd never found out for Jack Brodie about the marshal's deputy. Then perhaps none of this would be about to happen.'

Mel put his arm around her. 'Don't fret, Rose,' he said gruffly. 'I guess the whole pot was a-comin' to the boil anyhow. Maybe it's time fer us to light a shuck – to hightail it away from Antelope jest like we've bin plannin'. Could be we've sat tight fer too long.'

'Do you really think so? Honest and truly?' Rose asked, a little nervously.

'Sure. You're not gettin' cold feet, are yuh?'

'N-no. But it's a far and dangerous journey to California.'

'The dangers is crowdin' here no less! I

seen that federal lawdog, remember? He has eyes that look right through a man an' turn his heart to ice-water. I don't care a rap for Sheriff Randers, but if Cannon should start diggin' an' get a scent o' how we've bin buildin' our nest-egg, our goose'll be plenty cooked!'

'Because we've been helping Brother Pryor and his people?'

'Think what the cattle bosses'd make o' that! What your pa would say!'

'Most of the cattle you've "rustled" for them have been Crazy-P stock, Mel. There's nothing wrong in selling what's your own. And my father is simply jealous of Mr Pryor's power to spread the Word!'

Rose had let her voice climb to an indignant cry.

'Shh!' Mel hissed. 'We don't want nobody knowin' we're out here!'

Chastened, Rose lifted her fingers to her mouth. 'No, of course not,' she mumbled softly.

Mel moved her hand away and caressed

her cheek with his own. 'Well, what's it to be, Rose? Our game's gonna be up mighty fast, I figger. Then we'll be right in the soup.'

Rose's eyes were dark, wide pools in her moon-pale face. 'What d'you want us to do?'

'I'm ridin' to Jerusalem Pastures to warn ol' Pryor pronto. That an' collect the rest o' my dues offa him – tonight!'

Mel's voice was low and ragged with what he hoped she would take only for manly resolution. 'D'you come with me? Do we get him to marry us, like we've bin fixin' on, an' do we quit this dump for a new life in Californi' as man an' wife?'

Rose swallowed and let go a trembling sigh. 'Oh, Mel, it's everything I want, but you know what they say about greener grass, and California is such a long way to travel. Our kin would despair and declare we were a pair of silly young fools ever to try it.'

'We'd be worse fools to stay,' he said grimly. 'You ain't changin' your mind, are you?'

She shook her head helplessly, biting her lip.

''Cause I have to go, even if it means leavin' you here by your lonesome. Don't you see that?'

Rose gulped, recollecting the tedium of her parsonage life in a two-bit, one-horse dump of a cattle town. She also feared that her part in the unmasking of Yale Cannon might yet be revealed. What shame and punishment would that bring?

Impulsively, she grasped his arm. 'I'll come, Mel,' she said in a shaky voice. 'I understand everything you're saying – and I'll come!'

From his hotel window, Cannon witnessed the stirring of the uneasy town of Antelope. He heard shouts raised near and far, the slamming of doors, the running of feet on boardwalks.

Swiftly, be strapped on his shoulder gun-rig and shrugged his broad shoulders into his coat.

'Stay here, ma'am!' he ordered Kate McDowell. 'Don't venture onto the street till this ruckus is over – and it would be best not to show movement at the window.'

He turned his attention to the lamp, blowing it out. 'A precaution,' he explained. 'In light of what you've told me, it would be best if the room looked unoccupied, else some drunk hellion might fancy his chances of putting me out of circulation.'

Kate hadn't considered such a possibility. She was horrified and shuddered. 'Good gracious! Do you think this disturbance can be linked to the committee's business?'

'You never know, and I don't want anything bad happening to anybody purely on account of my identity being disclosed.'

Cannon raced out into the narrow hallway and plunged down the stairs two at a time. In the dingy lobby, the night clerk was standing at the street door, gawping blearily at the crowd gathering outside the neighbouring saloon.

'Shucks, mister!' he wheezed. 'I swear I heered shootin' right thar in the Four Aces!'

Cannon barged past him. Though the

crashing of guns had ceased, a wild sound of arguing voices swelled from the saloon. The whole building seemed crouched like a wounded dog cringing in the shadows at the side of Main Street, growling and gathering itself up for another frantic leap into gut-ripping violence.

Smoke hung in the pool of light that spilled over and around the batwing doors onto the boardwalk. From the acrid smell, not all of it was tobacco smoke.

Up the street from the direction of the courthouse and jail hustled two men. The bobbing light of a lantern one of them carried showed Cannon the tin stars pinned to their vests. Sheriff Willy Randers sided by a deputy coming to investigate the distur-bance, he didn't doubt.

The local lawmen reached the saloon just ahead of Cannon. They didn't so much as look at him. The thick-set, authoritative man with the red-blotched face and yellow hair bored right on in through the batwings, followed by his deputy and Cannon.

The air in the crowded place could be cut with a knife. It stank of spilled booze, sawdust, stale smoke and men's sweaty clothes. The atmosphere sizzled with well-oiled aggression. A hubbub of heated talk rose and fell and was much-punctuated with foul oaths and savage shouts of advice.

Sporadically, meaty thumps were followed by breathy groans as drunken punches connected.

Two men were on the floor, trying to hit each other, legs and arms writhing madly. The crowd seemed split into separate camps either side of them, and was packed in several deep to the walls from the boots of those who edged the makeshift arena.

No one lined the bar at the far end, but behind it a dour-faced barkeep clutched a shotgun. Cannon surmised this menacing firearm may have had a lot to do with the cessation of the earlier gunplay. Even drunks were apt to remember that sprayed buckshot was lethal and indiscriminate.

'Sheriff Randers, boys!' a voice chirped

over-exuberantly from the mass of onlookers.

'Shod Sheriff Randersh!' slurred another.

The two rolling fighters crashed into a table and it crashed on top of them, wooden legs splintering, spilled glassware shattering.

One of the brawlers tried to get to his feet, but couldn't stay on them and toppled back onto his opponent, who promptly bit his ear.

'Break it up, yuh crazy bastards!' Randers raged.

Cannon estimated the combatants and most of the patrons were well liquored-up, some of them the worse for it depending on their natures and their capacity to hold their drink.

Randers grabbed the fighter who'd tried to get off the floor by the collar and yanked him clear. 'What outfit yuh from?'

It might have been purely accident, but the unsteady shuffle of the crowd brought it surging forward like the flow of a tide. A great bull of a waddie with a doltish grin teetered on high-heeled riding boots and was jostled heavily into Randers' back, pitching the sheriff's stetson over his eyes and releasing his captive from his clutches.

'Gawd! I'm sorry, sheriff – it's mighty close an' pushy in hyar t'night!'

Simultaneously, another lurching puncher swung the three-fourths-filled glass in his hand, and a stream of fiery spirits sloshed into the face of Randers' deputy.

'Shee-it! Bump my arm, would yuh?' he expostulated to nobody in particular. 'Now look wha' yuh gone bin an' made me done!'

The blinded deputy bellowed; the shoving mob laughed. But it was a vicious, sneering mirth Cannon didn't much admire. Nor did it humour him when one lean puncher, cocky as a rooster and emboldened by the temporary blinding of both peace officers, aimed a kick at the sheriff's wide posterior Yet more mirth roared from the crowd.

The kick was undisguisedly deliberate. 'Hey, feller! You got a gall!' Cannon found himself remonstrating.

'Shut your smarmy face, gran'paw!' the

kicker said. ''Tain't none of your business, git it?'

Nobody spoke to Yale Cannon like that. 'No, I don't get it – but you get this, coyote!' Cannon weighed one hundred and eighty pounds and packed no fat on his well-kept frame. His arm swung back in a blur of motion, then a bunched fist hurtled forward just as fast to connect with a bonecracking smack on the chin beneath the lean puncher's twisted grin.

The sheriff's abuser went staggering back into his pards with a yowl of pain and hurt pride.

'He hit me! Smash the bastard, fellers!'

In split-seconds the establishment erupted into a rough-house and Cannon, the sheriff and his sidekick were caught in the thick of a punishing, all-out brawl.

Mel Perigo and Rose McDowell lit out of town stirrup to stirrup. The girl rode a brush pony Mel had bought off a disinterested nighthawk at the livery stable. It was not the best of horseflesh, but it was a docile beast going spare and cheap. Best of all, the dickering was done without bringing Mel into contact with his big brother or any of the men who ramrodded Antelope.

At a steady gait, they put the straggling outskirts of the town behind them. Mel's bronc, a leggy dapple with black points, was familiar with the road. It was not the first time by a long chalk that Mel had hood-winked his brother and ridden out to the Pryorites, sometimes to carry information, sometimes to sell stock over Dallas' head.

Eventually the rolling meadows gave way to a more desolate landscape. The wide valley narrowed and foothills closed in on either side of the ascending, zigzag trail.

Here was the ravaged earth of the gold-fields. Around them loomed heaps of spoil and blasted rocks, the blackened stumps of trees felled and burned in times past. It was terrain that had been reshaped and made ugly by the blight of man's fevered quest for wealth.

Soon they approached the dark, tumble-down outlines of buildings.

Most of the one-time mining camp of High Crossing crouched beneath a towering, fifteen-hundred-foot rim where a wild stream cascaded down a narrow defile to give birth to the river that watered Antelope's valley.

Atop the rim was a big mesa, covering many thousand acres. Part of it was grass-land, but the lately titled Jerusalem Pastures did not live up to the promise of their name. The tableland was poor farming land. Nature had been in a mean mood when she fashioned this rocky section. The mesa was riven by deep, treacherous canyons – and it had not been improved by the scars of more abortive mine workings.

Mel pulled his horse to a walk. The high moon, slipping off a murky veil of cloud, coldly illuminated the weed-grown track that was the beginnings of the main street.

Rose shivered. 'This is a hateful place. It's not fair that Brother Pryor and his folks should have been forced to establish their colony here. Don't you agree, Mel?'

Mel gave a shrug. 'I don't pay it no never mind, honey. Just what did they ever do to deserve more? Tell me that.'

'Mr Pryor believes these people should have a second chance,' she said. 'They look for a promised land.'

'Too bad. Mostly they're hayseeds from the East, a-hoein' an' a-ploughin' an' a-scrapin'. Brodie's pack of wolves is right 'bout one thing. This here is cow-country. It's pullin' a fool stunt tryin' to use it some other wise, like raisin' corn an' beans an' such.'

'I'm sure God calls Mr Pryor to do what's right for his people.'

Mel snorted. 'Pryor's bin his own man on the mesa. His beliefs and ways of doin' things surely don't square with your pa's. Mebbe it's fer the best he ain't squatted in town or on the best graze.' He frowned darkly. 'Even here, they're gonna give him a fight.'

Rose didn't want to cross him. Not at this

point. She felt nervous enough about the huge and risky step she was taking in his company. She didn't want to admit even to herself they might have their differences in outlook and expectations. She fell silent.

High Crossing consisted of about thirty structures – or in most cases the ruins of them. The passing seasons, sun and blizzard, had taken their toll. Tossed up originally in greedy haste to cash in on a boom that had never materialized, then later simply abandoned, the frame buildings had warped and rotted rapidly.

Strong winds occasionally swept up the valley and were churned into turbulence when they hit the mesa. More than one ramshackle falsefront had been toppled down over a sagging boardwalk like a doll house smashed to splinters by the foot of a child in a tantrum.

Few windows still held glass. They were just black holes in moon-silvered timber siding. 'Like empty eye sockets,' said Rose.

But not all the buildings were unoccupied.

115

Giving the lie to the aphorism dead towns never came back, the more solid places had been taken over by the Pryorites. Incredibly, the biggest, the two-storied Finnegan's Saloon, had been turned into a religious meeting house and place of worship – the Temple, Abel Anson Pryor grandly called it.

It was from here sounds of life carried on the night breeze, putting an edge on its chill. The voices of Pryor's gathered devotees rose in a dirge-like chant.

Mel, unmoved, gave a short laugh.

'The action's still all over to Finnegan's, I guess. With a mite of luck, Pryor hisself'll be leadin' ceremonies at the meet, Rose. Plumb pronto we'll be c'llectin' plenty dinero to make out to Californi'.'

8

King of the Mesa

Mel and Rose reined in at a hitch-rack that had survived the general decay and slipped from their saddles.

'C'mon, we'll amble on in an' listen to Pryor rulin' his roost,' Mel said. 'He has the sod-busters eatin' outa his hand ... or scared stiff of him more like. Rules with a rod of iron!'

'You make Brother Pryor sound like a – a tyrant!' Rose chided. 'Perhaps his followers find him inspiring. He speaks with a lot of conviction.'

'A tyrant, huh? Waal, ain't that just what he is?'

Again, Rose dropped the whispered argument. At heart, she knew what Mel said was

117

largely true. Pryor governed here absolutely, the supreme master in every kind of thought and action.

Pryor was the self-declared king of Jerusalem Pastures. He delivered the commandments, laid down the laws and punished the transgressors. He also collected tithes, Rose understood, and the menial, practical chores of everyday living were performed for him by his acolytes while he devoted his own time utterly to matters spiritual.

His oratory was fiery and passionate. Rose could not help compare Pryor's stirring brand of religion with her father's dry sermons. Was it her fault if she found the latter wanting and anaemic?

And how tiresome it had always been having to endure her prissy sister Kate admonishing her for her disloyalty. At her age, Kate really should get married. Have babies. Stop trying to meddle in men's business. Still, Kate didn't have quite her prettiness, did she? Which left Mel's ox-like brother the only probable suitor

Rose looped the pony's reins around the pole, lost in the thoughts swirling through her mind.

'Let's go then, Rose,' Mel said. 'This ain't no time nor place for dreamin'.' He caught her hand and together they stepped up onto the creaking plankwalk.

Many of the former saloon's windows had been boarded up while others had been partly filled in to make them narrower and fitted with stained glass, freighted up from a defunct mission in Texas. Flickering candle-light within seemed to make the figures depicted in the coloured glass take on a writhing, supernatural life.

The chanting had stopped and a booming voice was delivering an address. Like two thieves, they made a small gap in the heavy red blankets that curtained the open doorway and sneaked in.

Finnegan's former palace of liquor, gambling and wicked women had undergone a transformation at the hands of the Pryorites.

The main saloon still made a large hall with the raftered ceiling two storeys high over the central floor space. Likewise, a wooden staircase still led to a gallery around three of the walls, off which opened doors to various private upstairs rooms. But the bar counter had been cut down and raised into an altar covered with a purple cloth and brass ornaments that glinted in the soft, fitful light of candles.

The odour of burning incense had replaced the characteristic saloon fustiness of tobacco smoke and alcohol.

Rows of wooden benches filled the body of the hall and they were packed with both men and women, all hanging on the words of their mentor.

Rose squeezed Mel's hand tightly and they waited in the shadows just inside the blanketed door.

Abel Anson Pryor was a tall, gaunt-framed individual of about fifty, with a chest-length beard and a mane of yellow-grey hair that hung to his shoulders. He had beetle brows and his deep-sunk eyes burned with a light some called fanaticism. He was in a brown homespun habit with long sleeves, belted in by a plaited cord around his waist. He carried a staff in one hand; a Bible with leather binding worn and sweat-stained from ceaseless handling in the other.

From the elevation of the steps in front of the altar, Pryor declaimed a message thunderously to his rapt audience.

'Brethren, the Lord has sent to me his angels, again commanding I chastise thee in His name for tardiness and lack of diligence in seeking out His ark concealed on the mesa.'

From a few more daring throats there escaped a groan of protest.

It did not escape Pryor's ear – or his beady eye.

'Brother Smith!' he cried, pointing his staff. Mel thought it would have been of a piece with the whole theatrical setup had a bolt of heavenly lightning ziz-zagged from its end and struck down the questioning follower.

'Beware this righteous and wrathful rod!' roared Pryor. 'Live meekly like He says for men to live! Follow His commandments, brought to thee by His apostle! Devote yourself unstintingly to the work of seeking prescribed by our Redeemer!'

Smith screwed up his dirt farmer's courage and to Mel and Rose a pair of shoulders amidst the cowering mass seemed to straighten.

'God as my witness, we bin lookin' ever since we set down here, preacher,' Smith protested. 'I got crops to tend an' kids with empty bellies to fill. This locked wagon – this whadya call it – *ark* ... whyn't it bin left where folks kin find it?'

Pryor's tone was withering. 'Dost thou question the workings of the Deity? It is hidden lest it should fall into the hands of the ungodly. Inside the ark is a treasure of inscribed brass plates, like unto those I dug up in Arizona and from which I translated our Book of Divine Truths, withheld from the Children of Israel.'

'Fiddle-faddle!' Mel muttered to Rose.

'Shh! How do you know?'

Mel bit his tongue. Though he had precious little time for the rigmarole, Rose was engrossed in it. A long time ago he'd resolved to tolerate her susceptibility, since it meant she would be happy for them to be married by Pryor in defiance of her fool father.

Pryor lectured his doubter with a laboured patience that made it clear to the congregation that the intelligence of Brother Smith was on a par with an idiot child's.

'The original plates gave our community its fundamental laws; the plates still to be found will lead our chosen people to eternal glory. Is it fitting they should be left in the open for any passing sinner to find? The disused mine workings are a labyrinth. My vision suggests that perhaps the ark will be found there, even though this divine task may consume many months.'

Smith mumbled an apology. 'I surely didn't mean no harm, Reverend. Was there food on my family's table, I'd of kept my mouth shut. With a consumptive wife an' two sickly kids, lookin' fer arks don't come easy. Kinda ain't fittin'...'

In reaction to having suddenly become a runaway, Rose's emotions were already on a hair-trigger. She was moved by the squashed rebel's plight. Tears pricked in her eyes. Impetuously, she said aloud, 'You must have faith, Mr Smith. The Lord brought manna to the Israelites in the desert when they were starving, and someday he will bless you, too.'

Mel silently cursed. He felt like an interloper here and hadn't wanted attention drawn to them. Not yet. But the damage was done.

Pryor swung his best hellfire gaze on them.

'Ah! We have visitors to our sanctuary, I see. The misguided Reverend McDowell's pretty daughter Rose, and our young helper Mel Perigo. Step out of the shadows and into plain view.'

Mel cleared his throat which seemed suddenly choked up. 'Actually, we was waitin' patiently for an urgent word in private, Mr Pryor sir.'

'Of course, my boy, of course.'

The preacher turned his crafty eyes back to his congregation. 'Do you see what I see, my friends? Perhaps these young innocents have tired of the wickedness surrounding them in the fleshpots of Antelope and seek the grace of God among true believers in Jerusalem Pastures.'

He turned his look heavenward 'Thou will prevail, Lord, I know. Good always triumphs in the end and this is Thy doing, O Lord – to bring this couple as Thou has brought so many others who have renounced Babylon.'

Mel coughed again uncomfortably. 'Well, we thought we might like a word with your *own self*, Mr Pryor.'

Something in the youngster's earnestness pierced the armour of religious fanaticism.

'And indeed thou shalt. Who am I to deny the pleadings the Redeemer puts into the mouths of his lambs? Come, and I shall initi-

125

ate you into the happy throng of the saved!'

Pryor made an almost imperceptible jerk of his staff and one of his novices cried, 'Hallelujah!'

'Praise be to God!' said another.

A pianist began thumping the keys of the departed Finnegan's restored instrument, producing the notes of a hymn tune, familiar even though incongruously tinny.

The congregation filled its lungs and raised its voices to let the world know it had avoided the burning pit of hell and come up into the sunlight of salvation.

Pryor motioned Mel and Rose to follow him and ascended the staircase to the rooms set aside for his personal use. The room they entered was almost in darkness, lit by a single flickering candle.

'The jig's all up, Mr Pryor!' Mel rushed to announce.

Pryor's response was a short, curling laugh. 'What've you done, kid? Compromised the Reverend McDowell's daughter?'

Rose was a little shocked by his sniggering

tone. It knocked a first small chip out of her uncritical admiration.

'No!' Mel blurted, red-faced. 'But me an' Rose gotta git. I need the money you owe me. All hell's bustin' loose. The big shots who ramrod this country are fixin' on sendin' a gunfighter to settle your hash – an ex-con called Red Effingham that Sheriff Randers has locked up in the Antelope calaboose. A mighty mean man an' a pr'feshnul killer!'

Pryor froze, his face putting Rose in mind of a picture she'd seen of an old-world cathedral statue graven in chill white marble.

'Effingham!' he breathed.

Then his eyes rolled in his head and beneath his brown robe his legs seemed to fold under him and he prostrated himself with an alarming moan on the warped floorboards.

'Oh, sweet Jesus!' Rose exclaimed. 'What have we said?'

'Holy smoke!' said Mel less devoutly. 'He's gone into some sorta trance!'

His eyes fixed and staring but apparently

unseeing, Pryor began to babble. The words were un-American and meaningless, but they were spoken with ringing passion.

'We better go get some help,' said Mel. 'He's havin' a fit ... an' I don't reck'n it's a fit of orneriness!'

'No, Mel.' Rose placed a trembling hand on his sleeve. 'Wait ... I think he's speaking in tongues!'

It was a convincing display, broken up like a weird conversation. Hair prickled at the back of Mel's neck and he looked over his shoulder.

'Who to? There's no one here 'cept ourselfs.'

'To *angels*, I expect, Mel,' Rose said in a shaky voice.

From below, the muffled strains of hymn-singing underscored the other-worldliness of it all.

Come, you faithful, raise the strain
Of triumphant gladness;
God has brought His people forth

Into joy from sadness.
Now rejoice, Jerusalem,
And with true affection
Welcome in unwearied strains
Jesus' resurrection.

The Reverend Pryor came out of his reverie with a last choked gurgle, coughed, fixed his unnerving stare on Mel and spoke again in English.

'Thou hast work to do, young man.'

'Not fer you I don't. Not anymore. I'm takin' what I'm owed an' headin' for Californi'.'

Pryor looked scandalized. 'The good Lord cannot allow that until His will is done. His angels have brought me His message and charged me to give tongue to His sacred call to thee.'

'What the hell are you ravin' about?'

'Thou art commanded to return to Antelope, take thy pistol and execute the sinner Effingham before cock-crow in the name of the Redeemer.'

Mel yelped. 'You're crazy! I can't go

bracin' no gunfighter!'

Rose stared at the preacher, not believing her ears. 'Reverend Pryor, you must be mistaken! Mel cannot kill a shootist – kill anyone! Why, he would surely die himself!'

'The Saviour will protect him in His boundless love whatsoever comes to pass.'

'What about *me?*' Rose protested.

'Thou shalt remain safely in the arms of my own household. My four wives shalt care for thee until the good deed is done and thy young man returns victorious. Thou shalt be kept *very securely.*'

Pryor's voice was full of subtle threat.

'Do you mean you're holdin' Rose hostage?' Mel cried, suddenly acutely aware that they were a mere two against a whole community – owned lock, stock and barrel by Abel Anson Pryor.

Rose gave a wail of anguish. 'But supposing Mel d-dies? Supposing he never comes back?'

'Thou hast no cause to fret, young woman. If thy suitor is not back in Jerusalem Pastures before cock-crow, he will be assumed to have failed in the Lord's work and to be dead and damned and in no wise worthy of thy hand.'

'Oh, I can't believe this is happening! What will become of me?'

Pryor moistened his lips. Framed by shadowy beard, his darting tongue was wetly pink.

'If Mel Perigo fails the Almighty, it is ordained that thou shalt become His obedient servant's fifth bride!'

9

Outsmarted

Bar-room brawls were not a speciality with Cannon. But he had fitness and long experience predating his army years to aid him. Moreover, his opponents in the Four Aces

Saloon were either flatfooted drunk or his fist-fight skills had improved rather than deteriorated with the passing of time.

He was quick to dodge the retaliatory blows thrown at him by the pards of the sassy puncher who'd kicked the sheriff and called him 'gran'paw'. He swiftly floored a second man with a steam-hammer jab to the ribs.

The hapless man doubled up, scrabbling in the sawdust as he gasped for breath, his face going purple.

But Cannon had no time to relish his comeuppance. He was busy delivering a roundhouse swing to the point of a third would-be opponent's jaw. It sent him flying backwards, out through the creaking bat-wings a heap faster than he'd ever gone through them before.

It seemed like Cannon, Sheriff Randers and the deputy were bailed up by the entire rowdy clientele. 'I ain't here to go the distance with all comers among the local hell-raisers,' Cannon reminded himself.

To get clear of the smashed furniture and

fallen bodies blocking any path across the sawdusted floor, Cannon jumped onto a bench that stood flush beneath a side window, meaning to edge along it to the door. With his back to the wall and above the mêlée, he might avoid further ambush.

It didn't work out.

Randers, propelled backwards by the drunk he was trying to restrain, crashed into Cannon's legs. Cannon teetered momentarily, then crashed headlong through the panes behind him.

He landed in the dust of an alley, showered by shattering glass. The heel of the left hand he put out to break his fall was cut and another shard scratched his brow. But he was lucky not to break bones – or even his back.

Stunned, Cannon heard what seemed to be a crackle of gunfire in his ringing ears. They hadn't returned to gunplay in the saloon, had they?

No – he recognized the sound had been too distant for that, and it was not repeated while the yells, scuffles and thumps raged on in the Four Aces.

He rolled over and was up onto his knees, shaking the splinters of glass out of his hair and off his clothes, when the next fast-moving development occurred.

'*Mr Cannon!*' It was Kate McDowell's voice, someplace close.

He groaned his annoyance aloud. 'I told you to stay well out of this, Miss McDowell,' he said tightly.

Perhaps deliberately, she ignored his reprimand and mistook his groan for pain, which it might have been, partly.

'Are you hurt, Mr Cannon?'

'Yeah, but not bad enough to stop me being hopping mad! This trouble was just drunken rannihans letting off steam, I reckon.'

'No, Mr Cannon. I think not.'

Cannon, hauling himself onto his feet and dusting himself down, was brought up short. 'How do you mean – you think not?'

'Those shots a moment ago, Mr Cannon – they came from the jailhouse.'

Silence fell between them in the alley as Cannon digested the startling import of what the young woman had told him. The hullabaloo from the saloon had wound down into exchanges of harsh words and curses. Somewhere far off in the darkness out of town, coyotes yapped.

'What are you suggesting, Miss McDowell?' he asked, but already guessing.

'That the fight here was a deliberate diversion ordered by the ranch bosses. I suspect their committee has already acted on its plan to release Red Effingham!'

'Well,' he said ironically, bitterly, 'they don't let the grass grow under their feet, do they?'

Kate shook her head. 'I'm afraid not, Mr Cannon.'

Privately, Cannon was kicking himself. Like the sheriff and his deputy he'd been sucked in by the ruckus at the Four Aces, which he should have realized from the start had the smell of a put-up job.

More to the point, he'd had no right to

dally over his official business. He shouldn't have wasted one minute in this pitiful little burg trying to lay private ghosts.

'I guess I should have gotten straight on with my duties when I arrived in Antelope,' he reflected aloud.

Kate's perspicacity was of a high order. She cottoned on to his train of thought and seemed to sense his frustration with himself. She tried to ease his mind.

'Duties to one's soul are sometimes no less important than duties to one's nation,' she suggested. 'You said yourself that the inquiries you made of my father were genuine.'

'Sure. But I was also being smart. Too smart,' he said with a wry smile. 'I kidded myself I was using my personal affairs as a smokescreen to blind the hostile ones, like the Perigos, to the more relevant nature of my excursion here. That was unnecessary and unjustified.'

'Oh, I'm sure that's not true.'

He shrugged. 'Well, all I've managed is to trip my own self up,' he admitted before briskly changing tack. A man of action, he knew all self-recrimination to be an indulgence and a waste of time. 'I've got to get down to the jailhouse,' he said.

He had to confirm how things now stood, get to grips with the new circumstances, whatever they might turn out to be, and to try to salvage the apparent wreck of his mission.

'But you're bleeding, Mr Cannon,' Kate said.

'Stop worrying about me, young woman, and take yourself home out of harm's way!' he snapped. He looked at his hand and dabbed at his forehead. 'They're only scratches. People may be dead or dying at the jailhouse.'

Kate frowned. 'I hope not. There was probably only the night jailer left there. A harmless old-timer called Jarrod. I'll come with you.'

Cannon was opening his mouth to veto that idea firmly when Sheriff Willy Randers and his deputy stumped out of the Four

Aces. They shepherded onto the street two sullen, handcuffed prisoners. One of them was the little tyke who'd booted the sheriff's backside.

'Yuh all right, stranger?' Randers asked.

'Coming right,' Cannon said. 'Sort of mortified...' he didn't try to explain why.

'Much obliged, yuh hornin' in like yuh did,' the sheriff said. 'Them looked mighty unfair odds fer a spell, but the hellions settled down sudden like, an' we got room in the cells fer the ringleaders, ain't that so, Tom?'

The deputy, one eye reduced to a puffy slit, growled an affirmative.

'Mr Randers, I fear you may have more empty cells than you allow.' Kate spoke up sharply, unconsciously employing her schoolroom manner, and instantly had the lawmen's attention. 'There was shooting at the jailhouse in your absence,' she continued.

Randers took it like another blow between the eyes. 'Eb Jarrod!' he burst out. 'We left him lone-handed!'

Tom dropped a scorching curse and Cannon saw Kate flinch at its vulgarity. Pausing only to manacle their prisoners to a hitch-rail, Randers and the deputy pounded up the street, drawing six-guns.

Cannon shook his head, then loped in pursuit. He wasn't much surprised when Kate followed. Nor did he try to remonstrate further. Things were moving too fast to waste effort on lost causes.

Eb Jarrod was slumped white-faced, bleeding from a shot leg, in the jailhouse doorway. A strong smell of gunsmoke hung around the place.

'Bastards threw down on me, Willy!' Jarrod wheezed, his wizened features creasing with pain.

'Oh, the brutes!' Kate's voice trembled with indignation. 'I'll go fetch Doc Reedy for you this minute, Mr Jarrod.'

'A smart idea, ma'am,' Cannon approved. He unbuckled his trouser belt and quickly looped it round Jarrod's leg as a makeshift tourniquet which he began to tighten above the spreading bloodstain.

Randers rubbed the bristly hair at the back of his thick red neck. 'Who was they, Eb?'

'Dunno,' the old man gasped. 'They was hooded ... flour sacks with eyeholes cut in 'em. Pards of Effingham, I guess. They busted 'im out ... took 'im with 'em...' His voice trailed off weakly and he closed his eyes.

'Which way did they go, Eb?' Randers asked urgently.

'Uptown ... road to High Crossing an' the mesa.' He sank back on the boards with a sigh.

'All right, old-timer, take it easy now. Doc'll be here any moment, yuh savvy?'

Randers turned to his deputy. 'We'll organize a posse an' take out after the yeller skunks!'

'They got a head start, Sheriff,' Tom said.

'Cris'sake, there'll be tracks t' foller. We dassn't let 'em get away – thar's a deppity marshal a-comin' to take Effingham inta federal custody. Go round up some volunteers, Tom!'

The deputy shuffled and looked at his feet. 'Well … I can try.'

'Huh?' Randers' pale eyes narrowed with puzzlement. But very quickly he understood and glared with disgust. 'You reckon we can't count on help?'

'Naw. This thing'll tear the town apart,' Tom said balefully. 'That's what I reckon.'

Silence. Randers couldn't be resigned or reconciled to the notion, though he'd heard the towntalk and Red Effingham had exulted in putting him wise to the lay of the land.

'Hell, man, go and *try!*'

'Yeah,' said Tom thickly. 'I suppose we have to.'

Tom went and Kate came back with Doc Reedy. The sawbones shook his head and clucked his tongue and said it was a disgrace. 'Mebbe you gents could give me a hand to shift Mr Jarrod to my rooms. If the slug's still in there, I'll have to dig it out.'

Cannon said, 'I guess he'll pull through.'

'Hard as nails is Eb,' Randers remarked. 'Used t' be a buffalo hunter, freight hauler, Injun agent an' whatnot in his prime.'

They used part of the cot from Effingham's empty iron cage in the jailhouse as a makeshift stretcher to shift the shot night guard to Reedy's place around a nearby corner.

Between the jailhouse and the medico's, Randers again expressed his thanks to Cannon, and the federal lawman felt obligated to introduce himself.

'So my horning in, as you put it, was close to being in the line of duty.'

Randers looked at him amazed, but it didn't take long for his wits to gather. 'Yuh gonna ride with the posse, Mr Cannon?' he probed.

'Sure. Count me your first recruit, Sheriff.'

'Proud to have you along,' Randers said. 'Right proud!'

If Randers was encouraged by having a US

marshal's deputy to side him, Cannon noted he was also discouraged when they arrived back at the jailhouse to find Tom returned ahead of them, with a scant two volunteers for the posse.

Where the breakout of Red Effingham was concerned Antelope's citizenry didn't want to know.

'Those folks that ain't plumb vanished, jes' turned their backs and looked the other way,' Tom said. 'They got smart enough heads to know the big wheels want Effingham runnin' loose to stop Pryor's dirty work.'

Randers, bleak-faced, growled back, 'Tom-fool heads! Don't they savvy them as fight fire with fire is apt to git their own fingers burned?'

'So it'll be just the five of us on the trail, and myself in country new to me...' Cannon mused. He thought following the sign of Effingham and the crew who'd freed him was going to be a difficult task in the dark of night. Possibly a dangerous one.

'No, Mr Cannon. Add me to the muster.'

Kate's calm words brought gasps of surprise from the men. 'Perhaps I can talk some sense yet into the people riding with this dreadful gunman.'

'Now see here, Miss McDowell, that's plumb ridiculous!' Randers objected. 'This is *men's* business.'

The sheriff had used the wrong word; Cannon saw Kate tense up and draw deep breath.

'Sheriff Randers is right, you know,' he said quickly, quietly. 'These hotheads have already used guns and they plainly mean to force a showdown with Preacher Pryor and his colony. They'll not suspect they might be slinging their lead at a lady. Your place is in Antelope beside your pa, where the need for your services will outlive this crisis.'

Notwithstanding his cool reasoning, Kate persisted with saying her piece.

'Your opinions are outdated, gentlemen. No doubt you also subscribe to the view that woman wasn't put on this earth to vote!'

Randers, his mind on the more pressing

144

issues at hand, rashly confirmed her belief. 'Fer certain sure, fightin' is men's business, ma'am. A female's proper duties is to cook and keep house and have babies.'

'So many have forced her to accept.'

Cannon swiftly blocked whatever might have been the rest of Kate's retort. He knew they could ill-afford an inopportune raking over of what were probably old ashes.

'We thank you kindly for your willingness, Miss McDowell,' he put in as she reached the first pause in what sounded set to be a lecture. 'Fair-minded men agree women are their equal in everything except physical strength. And as Sheriff Randers was trying to say, it's on such account we must decline your selfless offer to accompany us.'

His dignified manners and his firmness on the point appeared to turn the trick.

'Very well, Mr Cannon. But let it not be forgotten that while women cook, sew, do laundry and teach children, they also think, have opinions, and are citizens of this republic, just as men are.'

Cannon answered in a soft murmur. 'When the time comes for persuasive talk, we'll be mighty glad to avail ourselves of your powerful logic, Miss McDowell.'

10

Scared Mel

Mel Perigo was in a state of funk. Cold sweat plastered his shirt to his back. The uncertain grip he had on the reins of his horse was clammy and trembling.

'Ah, Rose, Rose,' he groaned to himself on the winding trail down from High Crossing. 'The snaky bastard fooled us both! I should never have done no business with him, and you shouldn't 'a' bin suckered by his cant!'

Abel Anson Pryor had laughed in a harsh, sneering way at their protests over the ugly demands of his 'vision'. It was like the preacher had torn off a mask.

Mel now saw his thoroughgoing style of religion all too clearly as pure theatre – part of a confidence game. Previously, he had taken Pryor at face value: a slightly awesome, Bible-punching fanatic it did no harm to soft-soap and pander to, especially if it could fill his own pockets and help achieve his plans. But tonight the man had exposed himself as nothing more than a criminal, acting out a ruthless deception and manipulating people's lives for his own purposes.

At this point, Mel's train of thought ran off the rails.

If Pryor's religious mission was a fake, what *were* his purposes? And what was the attraction of the broken and scarred land where he'd chosen to settle with a deluded troop of obedient squatters?

Mel shook his head. 'It just beats all ... I don't unnerstan it, not by a damn sight,' he told the moon-stark rocks that bordered the trail.

But more than puzzled, he was afraid.

147

Afraid, and trying to excuse himself for a dereliction that would torture him as long as he lived. 'I'm sorry, Rose,' he mumbled.

The still night's answer was a jingling clink of bit against teeth as his horse tossed its head, a creak of saddle leather, a way-off exchange of coyote howls.

If the preacher-man had given Mel just half of the money he'd owed him, the kid would have been tempted to hit the trail west; to ride out of this mess right off like the devil was on his heels; to leave Rose to her fate. For surely Pryor would dare not act on his threat?

Mel swallowed and shivered in the chill of the night. Maybe he could. Maybe he'd *drug* Rose somehow. Come to think of it, the people in Anson's sect acted mighty strange at times, even though Pryor prohibited liquor on the mesa. Dallas and Rose's father said the Pryorites were touched in their heads by the contagious hysteria of religious fervour, but drugs might produce similar effects…

'I shouldn't think this sort of thing,' Mel chastised himself. 'It's wrong of me to figger on desertin' Rose behind her back. I gotta get her back!'

But how could he?

He couldn't take on the Pryor's colony singlehanded, and finding and killing Red Effingham before sunup was out of the question. The option of confessing all to his brother fleeted through his mind, but that likewise was unthinkable. Blood ties could be strained just so far, and he feared the thrashing his brother would deal him on learning of his treachery would be crippling, if not murderous.

Blinded by a myriad fears, stunned by the dirty trick that had been pulled on him, Mel unconsciously let his dapple take its own path, raising ghostly little puffs of dust under its hoofs in the pale light.

The horse registered an occasional snort of disapproval through distended nostrils at the late exercise and, as undirected nags will, it clomped back unerringly toward home at the Crazy-P ranch.

Yale Cannon returned briefly to his hotel room. He sloshed water from the pitcher into the washbowl and sluiced his face and neck.

The shock of the cold water took some of the fire out of the scratches and bruises sustained in the saloon brawl. It also tightened his nerves and jerked him into an illusion of fuller wakefulness. All to the good, for he'd considerable doubt there would be sleep for him this night and he'd felt haggard. Finally, he pushed some boxes of cartridges into his pockets before departing, toting his saddle-gun, for the livery barn where he'd quartered his steeldust.

The nighthawk was a melancholy roust-about of no particular notice steeped in the pungency of hay, leather and horses and with a left leg shorter than his right. He said meekly that he didn't know what the town was a-coming to, what with saloon riots and jail breakouts.

He spat over his shoulder. 'Just see'd Sheriff Randers herd off the prisoners he hitched up outside the Four Aces. Couple o' yahoos. No fair swap fer an Arizonan gunnie, I'd say.'

Cannon disregarded the note of censure, drawled a pleasantry and tossed him a coin. All outward calm, he worked swiftly, not wasting a single moment. For with each passing minute, chances were Red Effingham was making better his escape and plunging into new mischief.

He took his saddle, bridle and trappings off the wooden pegs in the stall and swiftly readied his steeldust. He stowed his big Winchester in the saddle-gun scabbard slung under the stirrup irons.

That done, he backed the steeldust out into the aisle and mounted up. He put a hand to the brim of his pearl-coloured stetson, tugged it down firmly and ducked his head as he rode out under the double doorway and onto the short ramp into the street.

The makeshift posse of Randers, his

deputy and the two volunteers were there on horseback, ready to ride.

'Better git on the trail,' rumbled the sheriff.

The five-man cavalcade clattered off under the cold eye of the moon and the somehow sneering gaze of the disturbed populace.

They had just ridden by the parsonage when Cannon caught a faint, muffled cry from the shadows behind them. The voice was Kate's, he was sure. He turned in the saddle to look back and saw her run out onto the silvered roadway.

She was wearing a gabardine riding habit and a flat-crowned hat.

'Mr Cannon! You will wait a moment, please!' she cried. 'I have to fetch a horse from the livery and come with you.'

Cannon pulled up. His impatience communicated itself through the reins to the steeldust. He wheeled it prancing.

'Miss McDowell, we've had this discussion already,' he began sternly.

Randers, reining in ahead, cussed at the

interference. 'Pesky female! Sich defiance ain't fittin'!'

Kate ignored him and ran up to Cannon who was closest anyway. She was in a state of perturbation.

'My sister Rose is missing,' she stated, oblivious to other argument. 'Papa is distraught. He suspects she may be gone to some ungodly Pryorite meeting up on the mesa.'

'Is that likely, ma'am?'

'Unfortunately, yes,' said Kate. 'Rose is still a child in many ways and susceptible to Abel Pryor's theatrics. She's also too self-centred to realize how bitter a pill this must be for father to swallow. Or perhaps it's adolescent rebellion.'

Cannon's brows lowered gravely. 'With Effingham and his sponsors on the loose, the mesa will be an unhealthy place for a lone girl.'

Randers snarled, 'We ain't got no time for this palaver, Deputy Cannon. I says we push on *pronto*.'

It was very clear to Cannon that Randers didn't want Kate McDowell along on a dangerous outing. He was inclined to a similar view. And it would have been easier to state it if Randers hadn't earlier worn his opinion of independent women so frankly.

'Is there anyplace else your sister could be, Miss McDowell?' Cannon asked, seeking a loophole.

'She might be with her beau, Mel Perigo of the Crazy-P,' Kate said hopefully.

'Is the Crazy-P headquarters on the same road as the mesa?'

Kate nodded eagerly. 'In that general direction, Mr Cannon. You could make a detour.'

Cannon turned to Randers. 'I figure we could compromise, Sheriff. You ride on with the men; I'll wait for Miss McDowell to get a mount. If we don't catch up, we'll rendezvous at the Crazy-P. If Rose McDowell isn't there, maybe Miss Kate can prevail upon the Perigo boys to help look for her at least, if not join the hunt for Effingham.'

The chance of reinforcements to his

meagre force was sufficient to budge Randers out of his obstinacy. 'So,' he growled. 'We do it that way. But if Rose McDowell's pushed on to the mesa – too bad. Miss Kate turns back anyhow!'

Randers touched his hat-brim and loped off, his three men stringing along behind in the swirl of his dust.

'Hard-nosed gent, but sound,' Cannon said, though the comment was to himself because Kate had already hurried off to the livery barn.

Kate was evidently a regular client at the livery and known to the crippled nighthawk. Her arrangements were made promptly and she was back on the street in moments, mounted on a handsome chestnut mare with a depth of chest that promised a stout heart and plenty of staying power.

It occurred to Cannon that the young woman looked similarly competent for the ride ahead. She sat the rented horse confidently, her slim hands holding the reins in a grip that looked firm and strong. He had observed before that she cut a statuesque figure – built on robust lines yet slender-waisted and neatly put together in a way that seemed naggingly familiar from someplace he couldn't pinpoint.

'Well, Mr Cannon,' she said, 'no use sitting here and staring about. Let's go.'

They did, and Cannon was glad of the illusion that he was taking some constructive action. But chasing across the strange landscape in the spectral light of a near-full moon did nothing to ease his burden of guilt. No matter what energetic efforts he made now, he'd been remiss.

Good God, he was a federal lawman, duly sworn in as a marshal's deputy to execute orders and processes of the courts. In this case to bring back to face trial in Tucson one William 'Red' Effingham, accused murderer. But he'd dallied, distracted like a sentimental old fool by the fancy that he could dig up a piece of his best-forgotten past. While he'd indulged his sick whim – fruitlessly – a bunch of misguided Antelope stockmen and their hangers-on had confounded his assignment. Chances were, the affair would now end in blood and death which would weigh even more heavily on his conscience.

Their horses were fresh and Kate was almost as competent a rider as Cannon himself. The night air brisk in their faces, they came on the posse inside of a half-hour.

When Cannon hailed them, Randers and Deputy Tom Tulliver were studying a mess of hoofprints at a fork in the well-used trail.

'Two bits says they'se a-headin' straight fer Jerusalem Pastures,' one of the volunteers offered, scanning ahead. 'Yuh c'n track 'em easy 'nough from horseback. A heap o' fresh sign.'

'I ain't bettin' on it, feller,' Randers said, doubt plain in his gruff voice. 'Effingham's a sly one. Slippery as a goddamned snake ... I shouldn't wonder at ambush nor nothin'.'

'Well, hell, it's Pryor's crowd he's gunnin' for, ain't it? Didn't yuh say there'd be no range war in this country while yuh wore the badge?'

'Still ain't no call to go off half-cocked. We'd be crazy to ride hell for leather into a shootout where we was outgunned.' Randers gave Kate a sour look and jerked his head. "Sides, we got a lady ridin' along now. We was goin' to the Perigo spread first, don't yuh 'member?'

Tom Tulliver nodded sagely. 'Yeah – too right. If Effingham's huntin' trouble that fast we ain't gonna get to warn Preacher Pryor an' his folks anyhow.' Another bright thought struck him. 'An' like Mr Cannon says, Miss Kate can ast the Perigos to ride with us. It'd be two extra guns, an' I reckon ol' Dallas takes more notice o' Miss Kate than most anybody!'

In the pale light Cannon could not be sure, but he thought Kate's cheeks coloured.

Randers pulled his horse's head around and with a touch of spurs was off down the lesser of the forking trails into a hilly wilderness.

The troupe followed on a narrow road that switchbacked over the rolling country, lined here and there by patches of spindly aspens turned yellow. In the mottled shadows cast by one of these unimposing woodlands, a tree had been determined to mark a boundary. Leastways, it carried a broken sign pointing straight ahead that said in letters writ with a hot iron:

CRAZY-P. PERIGO RANCH.

Cannon could make out the bulky humps of scattered herds of Texas longhorn crosses bedded down in the gloom on tracts of valuable gramma grass.

They finally reached the spread's headquarters, a cluster of buildings nestled in a shallow valley and pleasantly shadowed with mature oak trees. Hearing their approach, a dog barked and snapped on a long rope leash in the yard. The pale light of the moon made the beast a leaping silhouette against the whitened dust.

Dallas Perigo strode out from the sprawling stone home. 'Quiet!' he said. The single firm word of command quietened the dog and the ranch boss turned his attention to the unexpected callers.

'Howdy, Sheriff Randers ... Miss Kate. What brings you folks here – and so late?'

'A passel o' trouble, Mr Perigo,' said Randers, spitting the words past dusty lips. 'Red Effingham's runnin' loose, prob'ly with a soft-brain bunch o' semi-vigilantes an' in the pay o' big ranchers as should know better – Effingham bein' no more'n a blood-crazy outlaw.'

Kate took up the story in a taut, strained voice. 'And, Dallas, Rose has gone missing from home. We thought she might be here with Mel.'

Dallas looked grave. 'Why, no, she ain't ... an' I ain't seen Mel since he slipped off after the meetin' in town. I thought he mighta headed off to your place, Kate, but I guess I was wrong. Shucks, I don't know where he could be, neither!'

11

The Posse's Mistake

At Dallas Perigo's suggestion, Kate, Randers and Cannon went into the ranch-house. It was no more pretentious inside than out; just old and comfortable, Cannon thought.

A frail-looking, white-haired woman wrapped in a blanket slept in a rocker in front of a blazing log fire in the living-room. Except that she breathed heavily and rhythmically, almost snoring, she might have been part of the chair, her occupation of it looked that permanent.

'We won't bother ma,' Dallas said, and they passed on into the kitchen.

The place was basically clean, but less than orderly. Signs of prolonged bachelor management were only too evident. A shell belt was draped over the back of one chair; a part-repaired hackamore was tossed under another. Pots and pans sat on a bench, mixed with crockery that rightly should have been replaced on empty hooks and shelves. A cutlery drawer hung open, partly covered by a Stetson flung down on top of the side-board. A coffee pot remained on a cold stove.

The visitors sat around a table covered with a rumpled white cloth that had not seen a smoothing iron since its last washing and fully acquainted the Crazy-P rancher with the latest happenings in town, of which he already had a fair idea.

'What can you do, Sheriff?' Dallas asked, his brow furrowed. 'Where are you planning to go when you leave here?'

'I fancy Effingham and the gents he's ridin' with is bound for High Crossing an' Jerusalem Pastures. We traced 'em up to the fork.'

Dallas nodded, chewing at his underlip. 'Once you get into the badlands stuff, the tracks could peter out. The goin' gets hard and tricky. As a matter of fact, pretty dangerous country fer follerin' a man that mebbe reckons on pursuit.'

Cannon said drily, 'We figure this could develop into a three-cornered fight, Mr Perigo: us, Effingham and company and the Pryorite settlers.'

Dallas scowled at the last. 'Dirty cow thieves,' he muttered. 'Always was gonna bring trouble to this territory.'

'Old grudges aside, we need all the hands we can muster to side us,' said Cannon.

'I 'preciate that much, mister, an' I don't hold with no outlaw-led vigilantes. It's a fact they're openly defyin' the law. But I ain't got no stommick fer riskin' my neck on account o' hypocritical trash.' He rose and stood behind Kate, laying a hand without thinking on her shoulder. 'I'll offer to escort Miss McDowell back to town, seein's how her sister weren't here, nor my brother.'

Kate placed her own hand lightly on his. The instinctive movements were not lost on Cannon.

The woman looked up at the grim rancher, forcing herself to choose between his safety and plunging him into a deadly chase in which the fate of her selfish, headstrong sister could perhaps be embroiled.

'But, Dallas, I'm afraid Rose may have gone to one of Abel Pryor's meetings on the mesa,' Kate said shakily. 'Perhaps Mel is with her. She's a foolish girl, but she doesn't deserve to die! You wouldn't want that to happen, would you?'

Dallas' face coloured and his jaw tightened. 'Oh, to the devil, Kate! All right – you want me to ride with these lawmen an' look out fer the kids, an' I guess fer our sakes I oughta at that.'

Kate sighed with relief at the quick success of her pleading, though she knew it was only a small thing compared to the wider problems that faced them.

Cannon stroked his chin, partly to conceal the meagre grin he allowed himself.

'So that's settled,' Kate said briskly, rising to her feet. 'I'm so glad you're coming with us, Dallas.'

'Now hold hard, Miss McDowell,' Cannon said softly. 'We'll be plumb glad to have Mr Perigo ride along with the posse but it was agreed there's no place for your own good self on this trail. Surely you need no reminding?'

Kate clenched her small fists in front of her heaving bosom, but won control over her exasperation with men's minds set on flawed notions.

'Very well,' she flashed back. 'I believe you're all mistaken, Mr Cannon, but I can see there's no time to argue the point. I take it the road back to Antelope is safe enough for a lone female?'

'For certain sure Effingham and his new friends have already passed through that neck of the woods,' Cannon commented neutrally.

'Go back to your pa, Miss McDowell,' rasped Randers, making it a blunt order.

'I guess he needs you as much as us, Kate,' Dallas said.

Kate shrugged, as though resigned, but it was the firm, steely gaze of Yale Cannon that mostly forced her to swallow her pride. Something about this soldierly, middle-aged man was unnerving as well as reassuring. She sensed he had a will that matched her own too perfectly. It made her uneasy, frightened her perhaps.

'All right, gentleman, I wouldn't want to be a ball and chain to you. Good night ... and good hunting!'

Then she stormed out and they heard her exchanging brief words with Tom Tulliver and the two others as she unhitched the rented chestnut mare from a verandah post and mounted up to ride for home.

'Damned meddler!' Randers cussed. 'Fine, strong woman like that should be busy with cleanin' house and bearin' children.' He rested his eyes a mite pointedly on Dallas Perigo, whose colour deepened again.

'C'mon. We've wasted enough time on this confab,' Dallas said hoarsely. 'I'll go saddle up.'

They stomped out to join the others. Dallas, buckling on a shell belt and a holstered .45, ran across to a corral where the saddle stock was held. Cannon and the sheriff climbed into creaking leather.

'I figger Miss McDowell's honey-talkin'' turned the trick,' Tom Tulliver said.

'Huh!' Randers scoffed. 'Precious li'le smooth an' sweet 'bout the school ma'am filly. She almost done bullied the poor feller inta it, yuh might say.'

Harness metal jingled and Cannon was swinging the steeldust's head, about to spur away, when he spied something that quickly made him draw rein.

'Whoa!' he called.

Randers jerked his horse to a stop. 'What's on your mind, Cannon? We best git movin' lest Effingham's gang is aimin' t' ride straight fer a showdown on the mesa!'

Cannon's sharp cry and the respect he seemed to command so naturally, perhaps as the legacy of his army career, had brought him the instant attention of every member of the small band.

He didn't answer Randers' query directly but gestured toward the ranch buildings across the yard from the main house. 'You got somebody else hanging out on this lot?' he asked Dallas Perigo.

'Naw,' Dallas said, staring at the darkened bunkhouse. It was a log building, long and narrow and beginning to fall into obvious disrepair. 'The Crazy-P don't run to hirin' hands no more, 'cept mebbe fer an annual roundup.'

'It wasn't the bunkhouse I was referring to,' Cannon said, following the rancher's gaze. 'It was the barn yonder – the one with the burlap-curtained window to some sort of loft. I shan't point and I'd be obliged if you'd not look too directly.'

Dallas shook his head. 'The place is jest a shed fer implements an' with a big hayloft.'

'Hmm...! Well, Mr Perigo, I could've sworn my eye caught that piece of burlap up there tweaked aside! Part of a face may have peered around its edge, though I wouldn't swear to it, mind.'

A doubtful frown on Dallas' craggy features suggested he was half-convinced Cannon was dreaming. But as unobtrusively as he could, he took a quick squint.

From the way he stiffened in his saddle, Cannon knew he was surprised.

'Doggone it, I figger yuh're right – somebody must be up there. Reckon I seen chinks of light aroun' that ol' burlap – like a candle flickerin'!'

The others caught on to the significance of their talk and a buzz of excitement ran through them. Deputy Tulliver swivelled his head openly toward the barn. Someone whistled. Cannon knew if anyone was watching the possemen, their demeanour might easily give the game away.

Randers ripped out an oath. 'By God, Perigo, I reck'n the sassy sons-of-bitches are holed up right here!'

'Easy, Sheriff!' Cannon said quietly. 'We'll move off orderly-like, then hunt some cover. Let whosoever's up there know they're rumbled and we could be inviting slugs through our heads.'

'Shore, Cannon, but this looks considerable promisin'. Ain't no sense in hell-tearin' off to the mesa on a wild-goose chase. We'll storm the barn straight away, dammit!'

'Shooting wild might be a bad idea,' Cannon cautioned sagely. 'There could be a mistake yet.'

'Plenty reason to clear this up one way or t'other,' Randers grumbled.

Dallas Perigo had the right idea. 'We better do like Mr Cannon says, Sheriff, an' sneak up from cover.'

He flicked his reins and kneed his mount ahead to lead them out of the moonlit yard. But he pivoted immediately, circling round behind the solid-walled bunkhouse.

'Smart head on him, that young man,' Cannon approved almost silently.

They pulled up and dismounted.

Randers said, 'Less'n any guy or guys skulkin' in thar aims to bust out pronto, we'll have 'em boxed in two jumps. They'se blind on three sides – the barn's got jest the one winder to the loft an' the double doors frontin' the yard.'

Cannon mentally sketched a battle plan. 'I suggest we split into two teams, approach from the rear and take up positions close to the walls, flanking the doors before we start anything.'

Was the postponement of their departure suspected in the barn?

Seconds had passed and the Crazy-P home-lot was still wreathed in silence and night shadows.

An owl hooted in the branches of one of the oaks.

Randers drew his Colt revolver and hefted it in a big paw. 'Time to get this over with. Let's work up an' call 'em out!'

Mel Perigo had been sitting hunched and despondent in the musty gloom of the hay-loft when the posse had ridden into the ranch yard. Its arrival knocked the remaining stuffing out of his quaking body, leaving him aghast.

'Aw, shit,' he groaned, letting out his breath. 'Randers an' Tulliver – an' that sneaky federal lawdog. Kate McDowell with 'em besides. They'll be askin' after Rose, I figger.'

The kid was in far above his head. He was all of eighteen, but he felt as helpless as an eight-year-old. His trading with Abel Pryor behind his brother's back had gotten out of hand in a way he had not foreseen.

When he'd reached the Crazy-P, demoralised, he'd stabled his dapple out of sight and slunk up to the loft, unwilling to face Dallas' inevitable wrath. Here he huddled over the glimmer of comfort provided by a stub of candle he'd found, verily like he was scared of the darkness arid the scampering barn mice.

When most of Randers' party clumped with his brother into the ranch-house, he waited sweating with fear for them to come back out searching for him. He was in a fix all right.

Should he try to make himself scarce? No, it was too late for flying this coop, too risky.

As first Kate, then the men reappeared and mounted up, his fluttering heart leaped. Maybe there was a chance they'd ride on and, if things fell right, find Rose before he had to show himself.

Bits of their talk floated up to him. They were conferring about something, but his head was throbbing and he couldn't piece it together.

Maybe their visit wasn't tied up with him and Rose at all, but with the other part of this crooked business ... the projected release of Red Effingham. Brodie had sure put axlegrease on his words at the committee meeting.

He heard the possemen's horses set off out of the yard and the murmur of their voices go with them and die away into nothing.

Mel was safe again, as he thought, when the silence was suddenly split by three revolver shots fired quick-smart at very close quarters ... like right below the hayloft window and into the barn doors.

He jumped to his feet and out of his skin, bumping the back of his skull stunningly on the underside of the shakes overhead and skittling the guttering candle across the rafter boards.

Outside, Randers' voice bellowed, 'Hey, inside thar! Throw out your weapons!'

Mel's nerves jangled and his teeth chattered so he couldn't speak.

'Yuh ain't got a Chinaman's chance,' the sheriff continued. 'This is the law an' yuh're trapped.'

The man called Cannon boomed, 'Show yourselves – hands high!'

Mel finally stuttered in the darkness, 'I-It's m-me, Mel – Mel Perigo. God a'mighty, don't go to shootin'!'

His wailing cry caused immediate consternation among the force that had closed in to capture him.

'It's no more'n your silly kid brother, Perigo!' blurted Randers, highly indignant.

'Mel! Shift your fool ass out here, but

fast!' Dallas roared. He was plenty mad.

Reluctantly, Mel forced his cramped limbs into trembling motion, crawling by feel toward the open trap and the ladder to the barn floor. Cruel fate was about to blow the lid off. Everything would be dragged out of him now, for certain sure. His brother sounded real ornery.

Yet he'd no sooner started his ignominious descent than all thought of his looming comeuppance was suddenly wiped out. His hands and feet were frozen to the ladder by the next frightening development.

And you could lay your last two bits on it – it heaped a fresh crime on his spinning head.

12

The Back-Shooting

At first it was just a crackle of sound like someone trampling on dry twigs, making them snap. Mel peered back into the gloom, noting it had abruptly thickened over toward the window where it ought to have been greyer.

Then his nostrils quivered to the smell of burning and he knew the denser darkness was smoke!

'Oh, bloody hell! The blasted candle...' he choked. 'Where will this all end?'

All at once, little tongues of flame shot up from the smouldering hay. They reproduced themselves and grew with startling rapidity.

Mel didn't stay paralysed for more than two shakes. To save his skin he'd have to quit the barn faster than a jack rabbit with a coyote on his tail.

Oblivious to the reception committee waiting for him outside, he shinned down the ladder, but missed the last two rungs and landed in a sprawl, twisting his ankle. Ignoring the knifing pain, he staggered to his feet and limped to the door. He unlatched it with fumbling fingers and tumbled out.

Smoke billowed out behind him into the night. Simultaneously, a draught of fresh air was sucked into the barn under it, fanning the spreading flames above into a new dance of fury.

Dallas thrust forward, temper flaring, cussing a blue streak. He grabbed him by the arm, his grip a bear-trap's. 'What the hell've yuh bin up to, kid? Why yuh hidin' – and why've yuh set the goddamned barn afire?'

'Hey! Ease off, or yuh'll bust m'arm!'

Yale Cannon fixed the pair of them with his gimlet gaze. 'Better leave it, Mr Perigo. The whippersnapper can be chewed out later.

177

Less you want to lose all your buildings, we've got a fire to fight first.'

The point put, Cannon wasted no more words. He strode past them, silhouetted in the crimson, smoky glare, and swung the barn door shut in a bid to cut off the stream of air nurturing the seat of the fire in the loft.

Dallas' face greyed. 'Christ – burned out! That's all I'll need!'

Cannon had not acted a moment too soon. Even as the wide door slammed into place, a crash came from within. Part of the roof had caved in and under this new sledgehammer blow the flame-licked plank decking of the loft collapsed to the barn floor.

Flames leaped and roared. A column of black smoke rose through the hole in the roof and spread into a cloud, tinted orange on its underside by the reflection of the lurid glow of the blaze. Sparks swirled upwards like fireflies.

'Somep'n' burnin' awful fierce,' said Red Effingham. He tossed his head toward the skyline, throwing back the greasy strands of red hair that hung lankly about his pinched white face.

Jack Brodie, who rode a few yards ahead, looked back, frowning. The rimrock to one side of the gully followed by the trail was outlined against a pulsing redness. The moon that had floated above like a huge silver dollar had lost his luminous shine. It was tarnished, probably by smoke.

'The Crazy-P headquarters lies thataways,' he said. 'Could be the Perigos have gotten themselves a fire.'

The rest of the vigilantes – a motley pack of hardcase cowpokes and misfit towners who'd tagged along lured by the smell of excitement and easy pickings put up by the organisers – milled to a stop around them.

'These Perigos sidin' us?' Effingham asked Brodie.

'Hardly,' his burly benefactor replied. 'I guess Dallas Perigo listens too close to our do-good school ma'am to know what side his bread's buttered. He's sort of neutral.'

Brodie hadn't beaten about the bush when he'd explained his own position to Effingham. Abel Pryor's dirt farmers were down-and-outs, mostly living in tents and shanties on the mesa. A few, trying to prove up as homesteaders, had scraped together enough to build themselves more permanent log cabins, but they could barely afford the necessities of life and none of them had a prayer of ever making the kind of money the cattlemen spent in Antelope.

Moreover, the religion drummed into them by Pryor prohibited all liquor and gambling. Sure as shooting, if they ever got to be a power in this land, the holy hayseeds would close down the operations from which Brodie made the best part of his profits.

Effingham brooded on this but briefly before he decided. He was obliged to the hotel man for his jailbreak and the diversion at the Four Aces that had kept the sanctimonious sheriff and his deputy out of the reckoning. But he was still his own man. And it was only a question of time before he was a rich one, too.

'I wanna see the fire,' the outlaw said. 'I gotta hunch it could prove interestin'.'

His tone contained a hint of arrogance. He couldn't abide to be seen as beholden to anybody. He sensed Brodie's dismissiveness over the mysterious fire, so ... too bad, this was as good a way of challenging him and proving who was boss as any other!

Without pausing for further gab, Effingham laid the reins to his horse and dug in his heels. He went angling up the slope, picking a way between the boulders till he crested the rise.

'It's a ranch buildin' sure enough,' he said, scanning the sweep of shadowy country outspread below. 'That this Crazy-P?'

Brodie drew up alongside him. 'Yeah. But hang it all, we owe Dallas Perigo nothing,' he reminded him.

Effingham let a sly smile curve his thin

lips, taking pleasure in galling Brodie. 'Told yuh, I gotta hunch, an' I set a lotta store by my hunches, mister.'

He threaded a way down the far slope of the ridge and the bunch of riders tagged along behind, Brodie included, though chafing with impatience like he had a burr under his saddle.

The country was less rough, leading down to open range. They put spurs to their mounts to ride at a steady gallop through the cold and the darkness. The barn fire was their beacon and they swerved from a straight course only when ghostly bunches of brush rose up before them.

Effingham led them off the grass of the plain to a wary halt in a clump of oaks on a rise overlooking the Crazy-P ranch yard. From here, he spied out the lay of the land.

'By God!' he whispered thickly. 'It's the sheriff an' his deppity down thar.'

'That's helluva damned thing!' Brodie snapped. 'Smoking out a nest of cow-thieving hymn-singers is one thing, but us fellers ain't in the mood for no more going up against law officers.'

'I knowed I was right follerin' my hunch an' comin' here,' Effingham lied, pointedly ignoring Brodie's tirade. 'I figger we've run across a blasted *posse*. Ain't that luck?'

Brodie scowled. 'Luck?' he queried suspiciously.

'Why, sure. In my book a man makes things his luck, an' we'll make this ours. We don't want no interferin' posse tailin' us up to High Crossing, do we? Nor need we have now. Lissen close...'

Yale Cannon had divested himself of his coat and hideout gun rig to work with a will as part of the bucket chain formed by the Perigo brothers and the Antelope posse.

They strove mightily to contain the fire in the Crazy-P barn. Cannon's brow was beaded with sweat and his shirt was damp and stained before the last flames hissed themselves into extinction.

Nothing was left of the barn except a few

blackened sticks and a heap of steaming, smouldering embers, but the rest of the ranch buildings had been saved.

Dallas Perigo surveyed the damage with hollow eyes.

'Where's my brother? Why was he layin' up in there, the jackass? I want to know the rights of this!'

'The whelp reckons he's busted his ankle,' Cannon said. 'I told him if he couldn't help, to get out of the road, and he dragged himself into the house.'

'Let's git on over. After pullin' this stunt, the kid's got some talkin' t–' Perigo broke off with a startled gasp.

Whirling, Cannon found himself confronted by three men with drawn revolvers. Some way behind them, hanging back in the shadows, a half dozen riders sat their saddles, shotguns or rifles nestled in the crooks of their arms.

Randers, Tulliver and the two volunteers were caught equally flatfooted in the same circle of armed horsemen. No doubt about it, Cannon noted with chagrin, the hard-pressed firefighters had unbeknown been surrounded by hostile newcomers.

'Lift your paws an' don't do nothin' rash, gents!' said one of the men on foot. He gestured with the long barrel of a heavy Colt. Pointed straight at them, levelled, it was hypnotizing – an unwinking black eye of death.

'Effingham!' gasped Randers.

The runty outlaw with the unkempt red hair smirked, his eyes like blobs of dirty ice. 'The very same, Sheriff. Nice to see yuh ag'in. I see yuh found business out hyar!'

Randers' face purpled. 'Our business is puttin' yuh back behind bars, yuh varmint!'

'And a hangman's noose around his neck,' Cannon murmured to the sheriff.

Effingham shook his head. 'Uh-uh, tinbadge. I'm actin' in behalf of a vigilance committee that has gotten other plans.'

'The committee don't have official jurisdiction!' Randers yelped in outrage. 'They've broken the law, freein' a dangerous criminal – an' armin' him with a gun taken from the

185

wall in my own office!'

Effingham hefted the Colt and laughed. 'Yuh recognize it, huh? A mighty deadly piece o' armament!'

Cannon knew the model. It predated the War Between the States and was brought out at a time when Samuel Colt had no factory of his own. It had been introduced by a Captain Walker of the Texas Rangers and Colt had it manufactured under contract by the Whitney Armoury in Connecticut. The Walker, though dated, was a formidable weapon indeed. It weighed five pounds fully loaded, and fired a hefty .44 slug.

You didn't mess with a man who pointed a Walker at you.

But one of the posse volunteers didn't appreciate this. Or flatly didn't give a damn. Or didn't want to see sunup again. Or panicked.

He made a break for the corral where he'd earlier stashed the posse's fire-spooked horses. It was a fatal mistake.

Effingham coldly swung the Colt Walker's

muzzle and let the hammer fall.

Cannon winced at the ear-splitting boom. He saw the luckless posseman propelled forward a good six feet, his feet lifted off the ground. It was as though an invisible giant had booted him in the back. A shocking scream was wrenched from the man's lips, broken off as his face smashed into the dirt.

'You've murdered him, Effingham,' Cannon said, fixing the stony-faced outlaw with his accusing gaze. 'In the back.'

'He shouldna run, the damned galoot.' Effingham spoke matter-of-factly without remorse or conscience. Cannon noticed a few of his new followers shifted uneasily in their creaking saddles, but none intervened.

'Now I s'pose yuh'll slay the rest of us, yuh bastard!' Randers said. Anger shook his voice.

'Naw. I suggest yuh might like to stay here, lawdawg,' Effingham said. 'While me an' the vigilance committee's recruits kinda sort things out up on the mesa.'

'For why aren't you killing us, too, Effing-

187

ham?' Cannon puzzled quietly.

Effingham indicated the men behind him with a toss of his head. 'My pards here is law-respectin', sensitive bodies an' ain't fancyin' to kill duly-appointed tinbadges. My own self, I reck'n yuh're stickin' your beaks in where they ain't wanted an' I seen more men die fer less than I care to tell tales 'bout. But I'll let the fellers call the tune. If'n it weren't fer them I'd be settin' in the sheriff's hoosegow yet.'

'A very generous gesture of appreciation, I'm sure,' drawled Cannon.

Effingham looked at him shrewdly, taking in the austere dignity that came across despite the smoke-grimed face and shirt-sleeved dishevelment. 'I take yuh fer this gent name o' Cannon – the federal marshal's deppity I hear tell's up from Arizona?'

Cannon inclined his head gravely. 'No less.'

'Wal, figger on this, pilgrim: I might be feelin' public-spirited, but my trigger finger kin still have an axy-dent!'

The outlaw jerked his head again at his compatriots. 'Make 'em comfortable in the ranch-house, boys.' He sneered. 'But tie 'em up good first! We don't want no blasted posse doggin' us, do we?'

Some of the tougher elements in his new crew sniggered. Maybe aiming to curry favour with the ruthless leader they'd busted out of jail, they jumped to do his bidding.

Nor when the prisoners were dragged into the ranch-house did it take the self-styled vigilantes long to find crippled Mel Perigo cowering with his invalid mother in the living-room.

Effingham shrugged with unconcern. 'I guess we'll have to rope the no-hopers the same. Else they'll cut these cusses free.'

Cannon said in reasoning tones to the waddie who lashed his wrists behind his back, 'There must be a big reward in this for you, mister. More than meets the eye. It's something I'd like to know.'

'Shuddup, mister!'

Effingham, strutting the room like a

rooster, overheard. 'Let's tell the man, friend. Ain't nothin' he can do 'bout it, trussed up like a boar fer the spit.'

'Too right,' said Cannon remorsefully.

Effingham grinned wickedly and lowered his grating voice. 'Gold is what it is, Mr Cannon – enough to clothe and feed a Confederate regiment!'

13

Outlaw's Creed

'I knew there had to be something to bring you back to your old haunts, Red Effingham,' said Cannon. 'And it had to be big, or you would've cut and run after these poor fools busted you from the Antelope jailhouse.'

A couple of the lobos bristled, but did nothing, disconcerted by Cannon's cool manner and looking to Effingham for their lead.

Cannon took a stab in the dark, speculating that the outlaw's ego and the knowledge he was now free from immediate pursuit would loosen his tongue. 'Make some more talk, Effingham ... it's interesting.'

'You sure are the nosy lawman, Cannon,' the thin outlaw sneered.

'The law at your mercy. Savour it, Effingham. Tantalize me with what you've put across us.'

'I jest might at that. Give yuh a mite to brood on.'

'We're in a fine spot for brooding,' Cannon said agreeably. 'This gold is leavings from the old days, I guess, before the mines played out.'

'Sure,' said Effingham, throwing out his pinched chest. 'But leavin's ain't the word. It's a whole wagon-load o' nuggets an' prime ore sealed up in a lost mine shaft in the side o' the mesa.'

Cannon let out a low whistle. 'And you

know where it is! No wonder these guys think you're some swell fellow.'

Effingham was encouraged to brag more.

'No one knows more'n me 'bout the old mines hereabouts. I was at High Crossin' in the gold boom days, but when the war came I lit out to join the Southern army. Many of the old Coloradan boys were sympathizers for the Confederacy. Those who stayed smuggled out gold to bankroll us Reb fighters. But the Yankees got wise an' moved in to stop 'em. Tipped off, the miners fled with one last wagon weighed down with gold. But a wheel busted an' they was forced to leave the stuff behind, sealin' up the wagon in one o' the old workin's.'

'Hey,' Cannon interrupted. 'How come you know all this if you'd quit to go to war?'

'Yuma. Afterward, one o' the miners ended up in the pen, same as my own self. He told me ever'thin'. But thar was another bastard – a con man – what tricked the feller inta spillin' the beans to him, too.'

'Who was he?'

'Abe Anson was his name before they gave him a number. But when he'd served his sentence an' he got out, he called hisself Abel Anson Pryor.'

'Well, I'll be damned. You know something? I think I'm beginning to see some light.'

Effingham smiled thinly. 'Quite a surprise, huh? But hear the rest, mister. My ol' mining pard died workin' on a chain gang. An accident, they said, but Abe Anson was still doin' time then an' was part o' thet same gang. It makes a man wonder.'

Cannon frowned. 'If Pryor knows the whereabouts of the gold wagon, why is he still here?'

''Cause he jumped the gun. He lacked the savvy to realize them ol' High Crossin' workin's burrowed inta the mesa every which way. Thar's more holes in it than in a Swiss cheese. When he reached the place, he'd of prob'ly kicked hisself fer not gettin' my pard to draw no map. The mine names he'd gotten would mean nothin' to him, nor to most anybody 'cept folks who was there way back in the rush years, an' who's all dead or long gone.'

'That's how it is in these parts, I hear.'

'So Anson – or Pryor – ain't jest workin' this holy man pitch to grub-stake hisself, though it sounds a kinda sweet life... Naw, I figger it's a ruse to trick suckers inta scourin' the mesa fer the hidden treasure.'

'You're going to have your work cut out,' Cannon said. 'You've got to pull Pryor's fangs even before you can recover the gold and try to cheat the hangman's rope.'

The warning made no difference to Effingham's swagger.

'I'll be all right. Yuh might say I'm helpin' these folks an' helpin' my own self at the same time. I don't like nothin' 'bout Anson-Pryor. An' I got a simple creed, lawman – if'n I don't like a thing, I get rid of it!'

Cannon was relieved that whatever quarrel Effingham might have with himself did not appear to run deep. Effingham was more than just extravagant talk. All here had seen for themselves the outlaw's cold-blooded cutting-down of the posseman who'd tried to escape. Effingham had a vicious streak. He killed because he liked to, Cannon judged. No, needed to...

'And after you've killed Pryor and got the gold,' he said matter-of-factly, 'what then?'

Effingham's chuckle was pure evil.

'Wal, Cannon, I haven't rightly decided. Mebbe I'll take the lion's share an' jest hightail it outa this country, the world at my feet.'

He paused to gloat at their tightly bound hands and feet.

'Or then again, mebbe I'll sneak back here on my lonesome. Puttin' a torch to the rest o' this Crazy-P 'ud make y'all a handsome funeral pyre!'

With a chink-drag of spur chains, the vigilantes trooped out. Not much was said but the prisoners heard them climb into their saddles and gallop away.

'Good riddance to the scum,' Dallas

Perigo said with feeling.

'Ain't no help, Dallas,' said Deputy Tulliver, beads of sweat on his forehead. 'Who's gonna cut us free? An' yuh heard what Effingham said – he's a-comin' back to fire this place!'

'*Maybe,*' said Cannon calmly, heavily. 'My betting is he might not consider such games worth the candle once he's claimed his gold and dealt with Pryor.'

Sheriff Randers strained futilely at his bonds. 'I'd sure hate to be in Preacher Pryor's shoes,' he gritted. 'But him turnin' out a charlatan, an' a former convict to boot, I guess there's no call fer sheddin' tears. Even if we was able to do contrarywise, mebbe we should let the skunks at each other's cheatin' throats!'

It was then, realizing the possible consequences of such a clash, that Mel Perigo plucked up his courage.

'We can't do that!' he bleated. 'You gotta stop 'em, Sheriff! Innocent people c'd die. Rose McDowell is up thar at High Crossing

– Pryor took her hostage!'

'Damn it,' Cannon said. His mind rapidly absorbed the new information and its disturbing implications. 'Boy, we're hog-tied and this moment the sheriff can do nothing to stop the attack. We don't know what the outcome might be. But I do know you have a lot of explaining to do.'

With Cannon's stern prompting, Mel's story came tumbling out. It was as well Dallas Perigo was roped. Maybe if he hadn't been, Mel's tongue would have quickly seized up. Dallas' face darkened with rage as he cottoned onto his brother's duplicity.

'Yuh treacherous brat!' he roared. 'Horse-whippin''ll be no more'n the start of it when I lay my hands on yuh! Flesh an' blood yuh might be, but nobody pulls the wool over my eyes like yuh've done an' don't pay a stiff price!'

Mel flinched from him, white-faced, unable to look him in the eye.

'I know it was a fool stunt an' wrong, but I couldn't help myself, Dallas. I'd had a gutsful o' scrapin' a livin' on the Crazy-P. I wanted to start over on a life of my own someplace else.'

'Why'n hell did yuh have to twist your own folks an' grovel to thet faker Pryor, yuh damned fool?' Dallas demanded angrily. 'This finishes yuh, kid! Leastwise, it's the end as fur as the Crazy-P's concerned I'll get lawyers to draw up papers-'

'Hold your horses, friends!' Cannon broke in, his voice placating. 'There are more – uh – pressing matters before that can be attended to. Like getting ourselves out of this spot quick-fast.'

'Yeah,' grunted Randers. 'This ain't no time to get riled up over fam'ly diff'rences But jest how *do* we get outa this? Tell me that!'

Nobody rushed to answer. Dallas' broad shoulders slumped, bowed by the prospect of keeping the Crazy-P running lone-handed Then, into their grave silence, came the sounds of an approaching rider. Wonderingly, they heard hard-loping hoofbeats reduce to a canter and the horse brought to a snorting halt.

Had Effingham or one of his misguided backers already returned?

Light footfalls sounded tantalizingly on the boards of the verandah, and a female voice said only slightly tremulously 'Hello, the house!'

'Kate!' Dallas burst out.

Cannon noticed how despite the disgrace heaped on his name and the extra worries brought upon him by his brother's folly, the rancher's grimness seemed to fall away from him and he became alert, vigorous, alive. His transparent feelings were a deal more than the relief they all felt with unexpected release from their bonds at hand.

And Dallas Perigo's feelings were understandable enough to Cannon. The Antelope school teacher was attractive, intelligent and altogether desirable from a masculine point of view.

Kate McDowell hurried in. She gasped. 'Oh, my goodness! The unspeakable scoundrels – they've even tied you, Mrs Perigo.'

After his first cry of her name, Dallas Perigo had gone uncommonly silent and bashful. It was Cannon who urged Kate to get a knife and set them free, but she was already rummaging in a drawer with this in mind.

The Perigos' frail mother started to whimper, though Cannon doubted she was wholly aware of what went on around her. 'There, there,' Kate soothed, yet not abandoning her task. 'Everything will soon be just fine.'

The instant he was free, Cannon rapidly massaged his wrists to restore circulation. As soon as the numbness in his fingers subsided sufficiently, he helped Kate cut loose the others.

Dallas found his voice. 'Kate, what are you doin' here? You was s'pposed to 'a' ridden back to town.'

'Do I detect a note of reprimand, Mr Perigo?' she asked rhetorically. 'There's nothing I wish to explain. It's as well I pleased my own uneasy mind and circled back to the Crazy-P.'

Dallas looked at her aghast. 'You agreed to ride home. Yuh could 'a' bin in danger aroun' here!'

'I would rather not talk about it,' she said stiffly. 'I saw the barn burning from a distance and was almost here when Red Effingham, Jack Brodie and the other fools and renegades showed up.'

'Yuh might 'a' bin killed!'

'I drew back and hid in the stand of oaks north of your buildings. And following my own impulses has served you well!' Kate said defiantly.

Cannon intervened, anxious to prevent the conversation turning into another pointless spat when there was no time to waste.

'Fortunately things have gone right for you, ma'am, and thus – gratefully – for us. But that isn't the case for your sister Rose. We now know where she is. Young Mel went with her to Jerusalem Pastures, where she's being held hostage by Brother Pryor whom we learn is an imposter and criminal. A bloody showdown threatens, and we must take the trail to stop it.'

Kate's eyes widened in horror. 'Rose held by Pryor!'

'And Red Effingham and his cohorts baying for the preacher's blood.'

Kate looked at the others' worried faces. 'I don't want to believe it's true. But that's really what's happening, isn't it? You're not just spinning a yarn to pay me back for disobeying you.'

Cannon shook his head regretfully. 'No time to tease; no time for more palaver. We never could have been more truthful in our lives.'

His tone was level but hurried. Swinging on his heel, he strode purposefully for the door.

Rose McDowell was in a state of shock. She tried to tell herself her mistake had been in trusting others too well, but it wouldn't stick. At bottom, she knew she could not blame youth or innocence for the frightening predicament in which she found herself.

She'd not been totally blind to Mel Perigo's shiftlessness, nor his self-centred ambition. In a way they were two of a kind, and mirrored in Mel was her own rebellious jealousy of an older sibling.

Furthermore, her professed admiration of Pryor and his gospel had been as much mischief-making as anything, calculated to scandalize her long-suffering father and her loyal, capable sister.

Remorsefully, Rose acknowledged she had herself to blame. She silently railed against herself for having got into this mess. Her own mistakes had set her on the path that ended here, in captivity in an incense-reeking, tawdrily furnished upstairs room in the one-time saloon at High Crossing.

Rose heard a fumbling outside the door of the room. A key grated in the heavy lock. The door swung open and the smoky flame of the single red candle planted on top of the warped washstand wavered, sending leaping shadows across the peeling walls.

Brother Abel Anson Pryor glided in, looking to Rose in the weird light like a disciple of the Devil. He thrust the door shut behind him and regarded her with a leering, triumphant smile that in no way conveyed the moral rectitude expressed in his hellfire sermons.

Rose gave an involuntary shudder but tried to out-stare his gloating eyes, struggling to get a grip on her trembling nerves. Her pounding heart seemed to have risen to her throat, blocking speech. The protests she had framed died unspoken and she waited for him to state his business.

He said, still smiling, 'Well, my dear Miss McDowell, it lacks but a few hours to dawn, and somehow I don't expect we'll be seeing your Mr Perigo again.' He chuckled. 'I fear your beau has deserted you, young lady.'

Rose was only slightly surprised he had dropped his high-faluting manner of speaking. 'Your behaviour is absurd, Mr Pryor!' she said jerkily. 'I demand you let me ride away from here, back to my home!'

'I'm afraid that isn't possible, Miss Mc-

Dowell,' he purred. His eyes roved over her. 'I intend to carry out my expressed purpose of taking you for my bride. Mr Perigo – a callow youth, I fear – has betrayed you, but we will take care of you in our community with the greatest of pleasure.'

'I refuse to take part in this – this farce!'

Pryor licked his lips. 'My dear, you're over-wrought. Bridal nerves, of course. I suspected it would be necessary for me to – uh – correct something of the sort. But rest assured, you will be able to endure the rigours of our church's demanding wedding ceremony with equanimity. That is, once you've faced and experienced your worst fears...'

'What do you mean?' Rose quavered, her skin crawling.

It was then he lunged at her, hooking both his hands into the neck of her blouse and laughing in her pale face. Stitches parted and seams unravelled with a sound of ripping.

'Sunup isn't too close that we haven't time to overcome your virginal shyness,' he jeered.

14

'I'm Callin' Yuh Out!'

Tears of shame and fury welled in Rose's eyes and she went almost berserk, screaming and clawing and kicking. But she was no match for Pryor who slapped a heavy hand across her cheek and mouth, hurling her to the floorboards.

The hopelessness of the girl's plight was forced home on her. Breathless sobs blubbered from her bruised lips.

There was no pity in the bogus preacher. Grinning lasciviously, he bent over and yanked her skirt up over her hips with another rip.

'Please,' she pleaded, 'I'm not the kind of girl you want.'

'Ah, but you will be when I've finished

with you,' he mocked her.

Then, mercifully, interruption came. The faint drumming of hoofbeats grew to an urgent din. Fast-galloped horses had arrived in the ghost town.

'Riders! It must be my friends – a search party, looking for me,' Rose lied desperately.

'Search party be damned!' Pryor snarled. 'Who's yet to know you've come here, besides that fool Perigo kid?'

All the same, the sounds gave him pause and he hurried to the window to see what was happening on the street. He was in time to see the bobbing shapes as the horsemen dropped from leather and melted into the darkness among the ruins. They'd left their mounts down the rutted roadway apiece, out by the shell of the old mercantile.

For a few moments nothing could be heard from the room except the intermittent creak of loose boards swung by the wind. Then there was a drag of feet in the black shadows and a clink. Spur dangles? The sleek shape of a disturbed rat scuttled across the open greyness of the street.

A hammering at a door below shattered the peace.

Rose listened breathlessly.

Pryor had a few votaries who resided with him and whichever of his wives he currently favoured at the former saloon, to meet his needs. It was one of these choremen who opened up, grumbling.

'What's goin' on here? It's way too early to be risin' the pastor from his—'

A sickening thump ended his words. The gun-butt that had rapped the door was put to the same use over the protester's temple, downing him unconscious on the stoop.

From somewhere in the house, probably the staircase that led to the gallery, a woman's scream came knifelike.

Straight after, a man's harsh voice yelled from below.

'Abe Anson! This is Red Effingham. I'm callin' yuh out. If yuh in thar, git on down – heeled an' ready to c'llect what's comin' to yuh!'

Rose's heart sank. Thoughts of imminent deliverance from peril vanished like water poured onto burning desert sand. Effingham's arrival in High Crossing seemed sure sign that Mel had botched the mission assigned to him by Pryor. She shuddered, suddenly seized by a chill of fear that made her numb to the extent she thought she might be about to faint.

Maybe Mel was dead... Maybe she was going to die, too.

She was sure that hell was going to open up in Pryor's Jerusalem Pastures any moment.

To Cannon's frustration, the makeshift posse, augmented by the Perigos and the undeterrable Kate, was forced to travel cautiously after leaving the Crazy-P. The moon had set hours before, and the horses were skittish in the pre-dawn darkness. The trail was rocky and seldom-used, the footing treacherous. One misplaced hoof could bring a spill and disaster for horse and rider.

It was not easy for Cannon to maintain his

normal calm.

The life of Kate's sister and other innocents was in plain jeopardy. The scum Effingham was making good his escape from the law and had already embarked on a new spree of murder. He saw this as a matter that would stain his proud record with the disgrace of a mid-life failure. Sentiment, ill-chosen tactics, tardiness ... these were the things he had allowed to muddy the issue and shove him over, flat on his face.

A sober pensiveness filled his eyes. 'Who would have thought I could've made such a fool of myself ... an old fool?' he muttered to no one.

By his strict code, he had to recover the situation or die in the attempt.

'Can we go no faster?' he asked the company when they were into wild up-country. 'It's galling to think those hellions have a head start on us.'

'The game ain't lost yet,' Sheriff Randers said. 'Like as not, Effingham an' his bunch couldn't of made no better time.'

A thin line of grey stretched along the eastern horizon by the time they passed the first of the old mine workings and sighted the dark outlines of High Crossing's cheerless huddle of decaying structures.

Cannon didn't need any map or military academy course to savvy the whys and wherefores of the settlement's strategic siting. It lay dead ahead at the foot of a cleft in the sheer-sided mesa, climbed steeply by the old trail to the top that loomed some fifteen-hundred feet above.

Light improving, Cannon kneed the steeldust into a canter, leaving the others in his dust. Stark cliffs and stratified spires of red stone closed in and sped by on either side till he was among the first of the crumbling buildings.

From there, he heard the first crackle of gunfire.

Bunching the reins in his left hand, Cannon slid his right to his armpit and snatched out his revolver He swerved around the debris of a collapsed falsefront and cut through an alley so he was behind the main block on one side of the main drag.

He drew a great steadying breath. 'The shindig's begun sure enough. Lord be with us and preserve the guiltless!'

Jumping from the saddle, he hitched the horse to a massive timber beam, now rotting in a hollow. The bottom was possibly part of a one-time drainage canal where sparse regrowth of brush and stunted mesquites strove to cover man-made scars.

He scooted up the slope, his Colt lifted and fully cocked.

The scene he came to on Main Street was chaotic. From the sturdy cover of the old assay office, he looked out at a full-blown battle.

Though professed men of God, Pryor's acolytes had no apparent shortage of arms or qualms at assuming a militaristic posture. 'To some extent, it would appear the stock-men are right to resist these interlopers,' Cannon reflected to himself.

Guns were bellowing and exploding all

through the ghost town. The air was pungent with burnt cordite and grey with wreathing smoke. Bullets sang and screamed madly across the street, drilling through the tinder-dry boards, shattering the stained-glass church windows of the converted saloon.

A man – Cannon thought it was one of Effingham's ill-advised followers – shrilled his agony and folded up in a squirming heap, a slug buried in his hip.

In this near-empty town, hemmed in by its rock-walled gully, every bullet, every cry had its echo, intensifying the ghastly pandemonium.

Randers and the possemen came up behind Cannon, looking to him for instruction. But even as they arrived, the ferocity of the gunfight was abating.

Raking lead from the saloon and other buildings occupied by the sect members had halted the advance of the so-called vigilantes. They had been forced to back off to what defendable places they could find in High Crossing's tumbledown shells.

'We're none too many but there's enough of us to ring them,' Cannon said softly. 'They don't know our number and some of you can duck along the back of the contested block to other vantage points. Take no chances on being seen till the moment's ripe!'

After a brief confab, the law party scattered, scuttling to their appointed positions.

'Leave the challenging to me,' was Cannon's last low-voiced instruction.

Cannon scanned the street for the key protagonists.

'Effingham I see bailed up to one side of a saloon doorway; he can't move out and away without entering the range of the defenders' fire,' he murmured. 'But where's Pryor? Inside the building, I guess.'

The gunfire became even more sporadic. Evidently the warring factions had reached a stalemate, or close enough to it.

Effingham spoke. 'Pryor!' he yelled. 'Are you a-comin' out, yuh rat, or am I a-comin' in?'

Cannon judged it time to make his bold play.

He showed his drawn gun and part of himself at the corner of the assay office. No one spotted him; nothing happened. Steady as a rock, he swung the pistol up and blasted off a single shot into the air. Three close-spaced shots would have been better, but instinct and experience warned him to save his loads.

Then he called out in a sharp, commanding voice.

'All right, you fellers! This is the official law. You're surrounded. We offer you a reasonable chance. Throw down your shooters and hoist your hands, or we'll riddle you! C'mon – hoist 'em!'

Down the street, the other side of the saloon from Cannon, Randers barked, 'Yuh heard the man! Do it – right where yuh stand! Jack Brodie, less'n yuh feel lucky, call off your wolves!'

The motley bunch of hardcases, cowpokes and towners were stunned, Cannon could plainly see.

'Hell, I've had a bellyful – I quit!' said one.

Their accosters were the men they thought they'd left securely roped and out of the picture at the Crazy-P. The turnabout must be considerably unnerving for them, since they had no way of knowing the strength of the force which had released them was no more than the Antelope school ma'am.

Few of them had a taste for testing the ambush and eating its lead. Those who were simply ranch-hands, acting for bosses goaded beyond endurance by the threat of encroaching Pryorite squatters, didn't hesitate. They dropped their hardware right off and morosely raised their hands.

Brodie whined thinly, 'Shucks, Randers! We were only giving as good as we got. Fat lot of use you've been in controlling these rustlers and polygamists! They ain't Christian, I tell you.' Despite his protest, he pitched a sawed-off shotgun into the dust and lifted his arms.

Waverers followed suit.

But two of the punchers were the sort who inevitably showed up in frontier communities when trouble was in the offing. They got hired for being gun-handy rather than for skills with working cattle from horseback. Maybe somewhere down the line warrants were waiting for them and they didn't fancy being checked out by a federal law officer.

Whatever their motives, they went to use their weapons.

Boom! Boom!

Cannon was merciless His first shot took one of the gunnies in the leg. He was jerked off his feet, blood bubbling from a shattered kneecap. Flung raglike to the ground, he writhed and mewled helplessly, churning the dust to a chocolate mud beneath his broken limb.

The second shot, after Cannon had thumb-cocked, was not as accurate. It went high and hit the other gunnie in the head. A raw, red hole opened between his shocked eyes. He went down on his knees in an attitude suggestive of prayer before he keeled over, a dead man.

Cannon himself was not unscathed from the exchange. A bullet whistled past his head so close it grazed his ear. Another holed the flying tail of his coat as he flung himself aside to dodge the hard-cases' defiant fire.

Meanwhile, Effingham had realized it was do or die for him. Shrewd as ever, he didn't waste bullets trying to pot enemies seen or unseen on the Street. Nor did he stop to back the fatal gamble of his more foolhardy former comrades.

He took his chances and plunged through the door into Pryor's temple, slamming it behind him and stitching the gloom inside with bolts of flaming red from the purloined Walker.

Women shrilled; men yelled and cussed.

The blood dripped stickily but slowly from Cannon's damaged ear. He took rapid stock.

The cunning and competence of his assault had swiftly stifled the bulk of the opposition. Randers and the others were moving to round up the disarmed vigilantes. Pryor's adherents had no will to fight new arrivals who had possibly saved their lives.

It was time to complete the rout with the re-arrest of William 'Red' Effingham. Cannon ran toward the closed door through which his quarry had vanished.

'Effingham!' he bellowed in level, authoritative tones. 'In the name of the United States of America, I want you!'

Inside, three more shots were fired, possibly from two different guns.

Again, a young woman screamed.

Rose?

Red Effingham was fuming mad when he burst into Pryor's sanctum, gun blazing. His plans had gone awry with the intrusion of the beleaguering force led by Yale Cannon and the sheriff of Antelope. By Judas, how he wished he'd shot them both dead in cold blood while he'd had the chance!

But the game wasn't lost yet. The crafty, cheating Abe Anson – or Pryor as his moniker was here – was holed up in this place and would die yet.

And Pryor had evidently failed to find the cached gold. It would still be his to collect once he broke out of here. Yeah, *break out of here*. He'd pulled smarter stunts before.

Already he'd gotten the glimmerings of an idea. He'd heard women screaming in this strange-smelling dump, hadn't he? He reckoned Cannon was the kind of stuffed shirt who'd think twice about killing a woman

His adjusting eyes picked out the staircase leading to the gallery from the deserted main chamber. Around doors up there were cracks of light, tell-tale signs of where the occupants had retreated.

'Pryor! Show yuhself, yuh yeller dawg!'

Effingham's shout produced only the sound of feet pounding on floorboards, a knocking on walls and muffled but terse instructions. 'Get the scattergun – the ten-gauge! He's inside, you fools!'

Effingham snarled. 'I ain't facin' no Greener.' Promptly he fired at the door he took to be to the main upstairs room.

The heavy slug drilled a splintering path through a panel and a girl in the room screamed. Angry words were exchanged and Effingham heard a slap and a heavy thud, as though someone was thrown to the floor. The girl began sobbing.

All at once the door was flung back and a robed figure darted through the opening to the stairhead. In his fist was a long-cylindered, old-fashioned Army Colt. He loosed a wild shot, though it was doubtful he could make out a target in the shadows at the foot of the stairs.

'Abe Anson, yuh're a dead duck!' Effingham grated, and a tongue of flame spat from the muzzle of his gun.

Pryor twisted and flattened himself to the wall, but the skirt of his heavy robe impeded his movement and the bullet took him in the throat. Blood spurted, rapidly spreading a great mulberry stain down the brown stuff of his habit.

The sham preacher dropped his gun and

clutched his chest. Then he crashed down the rickety staircase headlong, rolling and bumping.

15

The Crack of Doom

Yale Cannon was within five long paces of the door to Pryor's headquarters when it was abruptly booted open. Effingham shoved through with the young woman Cannon had seen at Brodie's hotel and now knew was Rose McDowell. He had an arm curled around her neck and a Colt .45 poked into her ear.

'I've got Pryor's woman, an' I'm coming through,' he said. 'If anybody makes a move ag'inst me, I'll blow her pretty little head off!'

The harsh ultimatum caused Cannon to

break his stride, his face muscles tightening with anger and alarm.

'Let the girl go, Effingham!' he said, charging his voice with compelling authority. 'She's an innocent party.'

Effingham scoffed. 'Yuh ain't no sergeant on a parade ground, lawman. The hell with your orders! She stays with me while I collect the gold an' light a shuck over the mountains.'

'It'll never work, Effingham!' Cannon bluffed.

But the outlaw paid no heed. The girl was white-faced, paralysed with fear. He dragged her down the street to where he'd hitched the horse he'd ridden to the ghost town and used his wiry strength to sling her cruelly, stomach down, across the flat, Mexican dinner-plate pommel.

The wind and all consciousness seemed knocked out of her. Almost as an act of bravado, Effingham loosed a shot in the direction of the lawmen, then put his foot in the stirrup and swung aboard behind his captive.

He lashed the sorrel horse to a brisk trot and rode out, leaving a swirl of dust also quickly vanishing in the chill, lemon-coloured light of dawn.

'Let's get after the bastard!' Dallas Perigo said.

'No crowding him,' Cannon said. 'Remember, the girl's life comes first.'

Cannon and the Perigos took to the trail, leaving Randers and the others to keep the uneasy peace in High Crossing. They ascended onto the mesa to meet the rising sun, a bright streak at first but enlarging quickly into a dazzling orb.

Effingham had made good his escape into this blinding light, familiar with the outlines of his route. The pursuers were forced to rein in frequently and cast around for his tracks.

Many narrow canyons cleaved the flat top of the plateau. Here and there tumbling streams had been dammed and diverted by Pryor's colony to tilled fields. Tethered goats nibbled lush grass outside shanties and cabins. Cannon appreciated the worries of the committed cattlemen whose herds grazed the plains below. Water in this country had become more precious than the pinched-out seams of gold.

A half-hour's hard riding and fresh sign brought them to a spot where a weed-grown cut trail branched away under a clump of aspen into a canyon. They pushed through the lower branches, noting some were newly broken, and looked down on an abandoned mine works.

The rugged side trail stretched away by switch-backs and dizzying grades between slag heaps and dark shaft openings to shadowy depths beyond. A reduction shed sprawled down the face of the barren slope, along with a few other scattered and derelict structures.

Cannon caught a reddish flicker of movement at the corner of one of the sheds. In its lee was tethered Effingham's sorrel, its tail swishing at flies.

'Careful now,' Cannon cautioned, edging his steeldust back under the aspens.

'How dare you–!'

Rose McDowell objected to Red Effingham's groping hands as he pulled her off his horse, and was promptly clutched more tightly and pinched painfully.

'Ouch!'

'Findin' some spunk, huh?' he sneered. 'Why pretend to be somethin' yuh ain't? If yuh was so partic'lar, yuh wouldn't of bin sharin' a room with Pryor.'

The outlaw pushed his prisoner into a decaying mine shack, where he lashed her wrists and ankles tightly together with rawhide strings taken from his saddle. Rose retched dryly from the depths of her bruised stomach when he gagged her with a sweaty bandana.

He laughed at her discomfort. 'Now don't go anywheres, gal. Why, I might even be in the mood to do a li'le *celebratin'* with yuh later!'

Effingham left the shack and scrambled up a slope to a patch of scrub. He tore pieces of it out by the roots, uncovering the sagging portal of a tunnel. He slipped through the opening he'd made.

The entry appeared to give on to no more than a damp-smelling cave with a back wall of loose scree. Effingham struck a lucifer on the seat of his grubby Levis and grunted with satisfaction at what its flame's leaping light revealed.

Everything was how he'd expected to find it.

Stashed to one side of the tunnel entry on some timber lags were sticks of powder, some coiled fuse and blasting caps – put there against the day when the returning supporters of the Confederacy needed to unseal the inner reaches of the old mine and bring out their wagon of gold!

A small warning stirred through Effingham. He sniffed and frowned. The damp in here could spoil his plans yet. What if the many seasons' storage had caused the explosives to deteriorate? The caps *could* draw dampness.

He looked around and spied a wheel-barrow. Sun was starting to shine into the mouth of the tunnel. If he could move some of the stuff into its strengthening rays, he reckoned it would quickly dry out.

Effingham stacked seven dynamite sticks, side by side, in the wheelbarrow and set a full box of blasting caps beside them. He trundled the creaking barrow to the en-trance.

'It's gonna work... It *has* to work,' he argued to himself.

After a few impatient minutes, he decided to open the box of caps and make a primer – putting a cut length of fuse in a blasting cap – to test if the caps were good.

He split the end of the fuse the better to light it, and retreating inside the tunnel, lighted a cigar he pulled from his vest pocket. A stogie made a good wick and beat fumbling with lucifers in a breeze.

Cannon glided stealthily through the brush, working his way down toward the wrecked mine buildings, keeping himself concealed from them all the way. He had his Colt in his hand, for he knew that when he came across Effingham, more lead was going to fly.

Seeing no movement from the abandoned camp, he scrambled down the last part of the slope and made a tigerish run for the cover of the nearest hut. It carried a board that still spelled out in peeling paint the word 'Office'.

'Where for God's sake has Effingham gone?' Cannon mused. 'Down a mineshaft?'

And there he suddenly was. Standing at a half-hidden black mouth in the rock face framed by a distorted timber portal. Drawing on a cigar.

Unaware he was watched, the outlaw picked something up from an old wheelbarrow stood in the opening. He touched the tip of the cigar to the thing he had lifted. Cannon strained forward and saw from the splutter of sparks that it was a fuse.

But his desire to figure out what Effingham was up to also exposed him.

The instant Effingham glimpsed Cannon peering at him from alongside the hut, he dropped the cigar and whipped up the Walker from its tied-down leather holster.

They fired simultaneously, the two shots crashing out in the stillness and putting plovers and larks to protesting flight from trees and crannies all around.

Neither bullet found its mark, and before either could let a hammer fall again, the shootout was brought to a hellish termination.

His attention diverted by Cannon, Effingham had forgotten the spitting fuse in his left hand. He passed it, trailing sparks, over the open box of caps. The falling orange shower was all it took to detonate the caps; they in turn set off the seven sticks of dynamite.

Cannon saw Effingham's face contorted with horror a split second before it disintegrated into a bloody pulp. His broken body was picked up and hurled backward by the massive blast.

The sudden boom of concussion knocked Cannon down, deafening him, tearing off his coat and shirt, skimming his hat high in the air. It was like he'd been bowled by a charging bull.

A shower of rock fragments pummelled down on his bared back. The bull had been transmogrified into a lunatic masseur.

Finally the din subsided and he rolled over and pushed up onto his forearms. His head still rang and his whole body ached. But he was alive and he could see.

The place where Effingham had stood was enveloped in a turbulent cloud of smoke and dust which cleared to reveal a bank of evenly-sized chunks of rock debris. A huge slag heap.

'No mine, no Effingham,' Cannon whispered through gritty lips. 'The crack of doom.'

It was a full two days later and Yale Cannon was anxious to pull up stakes and head back to Arizona.

The showdown at High Crossing and the explosion at the abandoned mine had largely polished off the affair. His bruises had left him a mite stiff and his nicked ear was sore, but he'd survived many worse injuries, and he was a tough specimen despite his passing of what many regarded as a man's prime years.

Effingham's slipping from his grasp had been regrettable. But it was over and done, and on full reflection the end result would surely have been no different had Effingham lived to be escorted to his trial and the gallows.

Time and again, Cannon found his errant thoughts turning to the other, private business that he had attempted to pursue here. Unbidden, his mind kept dwelling on the mystery of the Bell family and his young love Jane who had come to this place called Antelope and vanished off the face of the earth.

If Cannon found himself saddened, the

reverse was true of the Reverend Ephraim McDowell. The old minister was as joyous as the father of the Prodigal Son over Rose's safe return and her consequent realization and confession of her waywardness.

'This thy sister was dead, and is alive again; and was lost and is found,' McDowell told the kind and level-headed Kate, who unlike the older sibling in the biblical story, was happy to share in his rejoicing.

'I don't know about "musick and dancing",' she said, 'but if we're going to "kill the fatted calf and eat and be merry", I suggest we should invite Mr Cannon to join our celebration. After all, we're largely indebted to him for the happy outcome.'

So Cannon came to dinner at the parsonage on his last evening in Antelope.

Afterward, when the girls had turned down the lamps to a mellow glow and departed to the kitchen to wash dishes, leaving the men to their talk, it was McDowell who broached the topic of the Bells.

Cannon started, for as his eyes followed

the lovely Kate, envying the minister his caring household, the very same subject had just flitted again into his own mind.

'I thought that was a – ah – forbidden business,' Cannon said, a little surprised.

'It was,' the old man said, shifting the heavy-lensed spectacles on the bridge of his nose and blinking his rheumy eyes. 'But by no higher authority than myself, though I believe I tried to put it another way. A false way. You see, I, too, have committed a sin. Of selfishness.'

He paused with a heavy sigh. Cannon waited, oddly breathless, expectant.

'I misled you, Mr Cannon. The Bells did come here all those years ago. A father and mother, and their one daughter, who was a widow, they said, with a girl-baby still at the breast.'

Cannon frowned. 'Jane – a widow?'

'Jane was indeed the young mother's name. There was no sign of a father to the child, and they *said* she was a widow. But, alas, her sorrows were not destined to be with her long. After the Sand Creek Massacre, Old Antelope was burned to the ground twice by the avenging Cheyenne. The Bells were among those murdered – all except the small one.'

'The baby!' Cannon said. His anxiety to know was unbearable. 'What became of the little girl?'

'My wife and I, being childless and wanting family, adopted her to raise as our own. Not long after, Rose was conceived, but after her birth my wife sickened and died and the two girls were all I had – all I *have*. Kate has never been told the heartbreaking secrets of her origins, and rightly or wrongly I will strive to the day I die to keep it that way.'

A strange excitement sang in Cannon's nerves. 'Thanks for telling me.'

'You are an honourable man, Mr Cannon – an officer, a gentleman. That is why I trust you with the story, and because I owe it to you for restoring Rose, my own blood, to me.'

Cannon's heart thumped in his chest like he'd run a marathon. He couldn't speak.

A pine log shifted in the grate. The busy clatter of dishes and the happy sound of girls' chat came from the kitchen. The reverend felt it incumbent on him to continue as the silence stretched between them.

'I watched my girls grow up, Mr Cannon. I saw natural childish selfishness die in Kate and mature in Rose. I came to know the steadfastness and loyalty of the one – and the self-centred vanity and mischievousness of the other. Being a man, I'd not known how to correct the rebelliousness in Rose's nature, and so that wildness took its grip and ran its obstinate course until now her eyes have been opened to the purgatory that waits for all sinners.'

Cannon nodded. A lump was in his throat, but he managed to say, 'I think they have, Mr McDowell'

'But Kate will always be the rock on whom myself and Antelope will rely. You won't try to roll that rock from its firm foundations,

236

will you, Mr Cannon?'

Cannon shook his head. 'No, never.'

How could he take away the comfort and support of an old man's last years?

How could he say anything that might disturb Kate's happiness, loosen the ties between herself and the widowed old minister she'd always called father?

He had no right. And he'd left it way too late to earn any such.

Next day, when he made his leave-taking, Kate threw her arms around Cannon's neck in an uncharacteristic display of womanly emotion and kissed his cheek.

'Thank you!' she breathed 'You'll be remembered in Antelope not for the fighting and deaths, but for the lives you saved from Satan!'

After the single, swift outpour, she stepped back, tall and solemnly beautiful, serene as a mountain lake.

Then, his eyes fixed ahead, quiet and grave, Cannon hit the lonesome trail back to the south-west.

A straight, soldierly figure, he looked as though he rode with purpose. And only he knew the acid-burning hurt of it, and that he didn't dare look back.

The publishers hope that this book has given you enjoyable reading. Large Print Books are especially designed to be as easy to see and hold as possible. If you wish a complete list of our books please ask at your local library or write directly to:

Dales Large Print Books
Magna House, Long Preston,
Skipton, North Yorkshire.
BD23 4ND

This Large Print Book, for people
who cannot read normal print,
is published under the auspices of
THE ULVERSCROFT FOUNDATION